JUN 06 2007

Bridal Trap

*Also by Lorena McCourtney
in Large Print:*

Escape

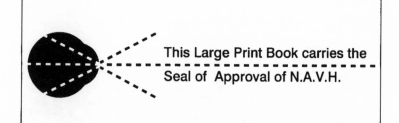

This Large Print Book carries the
Seal of Approval of N.A.V.H.

Bridal Trap

Lorena McCourtney

Thorndike Press • Waterville, Maine

Published in 2002 by arrangement with Maureen Moran Agency.

Thorndike Press Large Print Candlelight Series.

The tree indicium is a trademark of Thorndike Press.

The text of this Large Print edition is unabridged.
Other aspects of the book may vary from the original edition.

Set in 16 pt. Plantin by Christina S. Huff.

Printed in the United States on permanent paper.

Library of Congress Cataloging-in-Publication Data

McCourtney, Lorena.
    Bridal trap / Lorena McCourtney.
        p. cm.
    ISBN 0-7862-3833-X (lg. print : hc : alk. paper)
    1. Celebrities — Fiction.   2. Grandmothers — Fiction.
    3. Deception — Fiction.   4. Weddings — Fiction.
    PS3563.C3449B75 2002
                                            2001056304

Bridal Trap

Chapter One

Robyn Christopher clutched the brim of the old rain hat with both hands, pulling it down to protect her ears from the driving rain. She ducked under the leaky gutter that edged the old-fashioned front porch and turned to look at the storm that was churning the usually serene little bay into a surging, pounding cauldron.

Not a boat moved on those waters. Not a car moved on Main Street either, she noted. The only movement was a faded "Welcome to Caverna Bay" banner flapping in the wind. At least half the businesses were closed on this stormy Monday, several of them for the entire season, their owners fleeing to some sunny retreat in the southern part of the state or Arizona or Mexico.

Not Robyn. The storm made her feel buoyant, alive. This was the time of year she loved best, after the summer tourists had gone, after the snobbish residents on the south side of the bay boarded up their fancy summer homes and went away. Not that she disliked the tourists, she assured herself.

After all, her very livelihood depended upon them. But it was nice when they were gone and the little northern California coastal resort town could be itself again. Robyn felt as if it were *her* town now, a thought, she knew, that would probably appall some of the real old-timers who considered her few years here a mere spit in the wind.

Robyn slapped the rain hat against her yellow slicker and shook her soft brown hair free. She sniffed the fresh, clean scent of the rainswept air appreciatively before turning to knock on the weather-beaten door.

"Are you in there, Mrs. Barrone?" she called, pushing the door open a few inches without waiting for an answer.

"I was going dancing but my new shoes didn't arrive from Paris so I had to cancel," Mrs. Barrone answered tartly from her chair set close to the new stove.

Robyn laughed, pleased that her elderly friend was in such good spirits. Not that Mrs. Barrone ever complained, of course, but sometimes the pain of her ever present arthritis took the tartness from her tongue. Robyn slipped out of the shapeless yellow slicker, revealing a slim figure in jeans and ribbed, cranberry-red sweater.

"What can I do for you today?" Robyn questioned briskly, deliberately ignoring the

8

open scrapbook spread on Mrs. Barrone's lap. "Do you need anything from the store?"

"I don't think so, dear. I put a stew on to simmer a bit earlier. You might move the English ivy over closer to the window. It's looking a bit peaked," Mrs. Barrone said absently. "But don't bother with that now. I have some wonderful news!"

"Oh? Did your grandson win another award or something?" Robyn couldn't keep the faintly caustic bite out of her voice. She moved the asparagus fern away from the window to make room for the English ivy. Mrs. Barrone loved plants, but her small, dark house had little window space and she was forever rotating the pots to assure each plant a share of light.

"He's coming here." Mrs. Barrone's voice quivered with excitement. "Trevor is coming *here!*"

Robyn stopped short, the ivy pot in her hands. "What makes you think so?" she asked dubiously.

Mrs. Barrone waved a sheet of paper with her veined hand. "Because I have a letter right here that says he's coming."

Robyn set the pot on the window sill, squeezing it in between the curly coleus and a prickly cactus. "Does he say when?" she asked. The tendrils of a hanging purple velvet plant caught in her hair and she carefully untangled them.

Mrs. Barrone inspected the typewritten sheet again. "No, not exactly," she admitted. "Just as soon as he can get away for a few days."

Robyn hesitated, trying to think what to say that would prepare Mrs. Barrone for disappointment without letting her down too abruptly.

Mrs. Barrone noted the hesitation and glanced at Robyn sharply. "You don't think he'll come, do you?"

"I'm sure he'd like to come," Robyn said evasively. "But he's a very busy man. There must be meetings with producers and directors and publishers and all that sort of thing." To say nothing of escorting voluptuous young starlets around, she added scornfully to herself, remembering a Hollywood gossip column clipping Mrs. Barrone had found.

Mrs. Barrone sighed in exasperation. "You don't like him, do you? Would you like to read his letter?"

"No, thank you." Robyn perched on the edge of the sagging sofa across from Mrs. Barrone's rocking chair. She had no doubt that Trevor Barrone's letter was as fascinating as his best-selling book had been. He probably wrote the letter with the thought in mind that someday it would be auctioned off at some fabulous price, as the letters of the famous often were, she thought cynically. She started to protest to Mrs. Barrone that she couldn't really dislike the man when she didn't even know him, but she closed her mouth. She *didn't* know Trevor Barrone and she *did* dislike him. She tried to change the subject.

"I think I'll go down to the beach tomorrow. After this storm there should be lots of good stuff washed in. Did I tell you Larry brought me orders for two dozen of my driftwood mobiles from a gift shop down south?"

Mrs. Barrone's attention refused to be diverted. After a murmured, "That's nice, dear," she added, "but I can't see why you dislike him so much. Sometimes you act as if he had done something to you personally."

In a way, he had, Robyn thought. He had neglected and ignored this dear old lady whom Robyn loved almost as if she were her own grandmother. And now he was setting Mrs. Barrone up for further disappointment, telling her he would come to visit as soon as he could get away for a few days when he never really intended to come at all.

11

Grudgingly Robyn had to admit Trevor Barrone hadn't completely ignored his grandmother the last year or so. It was the money he sent that had paid for the new stove that kept the little house cozy and comfortable. The oversized color television set was a gift from him too, but if he had bothered to get acquainted with his grandmother he would have known that a nice little portable set would have been much more suitable than the big, awkward console model. It seemed to take up half the tiny living room.

Finally Robyn said carefully, "I just don't think he's treated you right."

"He sends money —"

"Money isn't everything!"

"As you pointed out, he's a very busy man," Mrs. Barrone said. Her voice, as usual when she spoke about her grandson, was completely without criticism or condemnation for all the years he had ignored her. "And after all the terrible experiences he went through in Africa, I'm sure he deserves a little pleasure in life."

Terrible experiences indeed, Robyn sniffed to herself. He'd made a mint writing about them and they were probably more fiction than truth anyway. And if the real life Mia looked anything like the movie screen Mia, his

12

"terrible experiences" had not been without their rewards.

"Oh my, I got so excited about Trevor's letter that I almost forgot something almost as important," Mrs. Barrone said, feeling around in the folds of her lap robe. "I have a new picture!"

"Trevor sent you a picture?" Robyn asked in surprise.

"No, no. Mabel brought it over. She reads all those movie magazines, you know. Buys them secondhand in Eureka. She brought this over just this morning." Mrs. Barrone thrust the clipping at Robyn.

In spite of her disdain for the man, Robyn couldn't help being curious. Reluctantly she reached across the worn rug for the clipping.

The photo had been taken from a low angle, obviously concentrating more on the curves of the young woman than on the man almost in shadow behind her. But enough of him was visible to show darkly handsome features, flashing smile and neatly trimmed beard. Stereotype of the successful young author, Robyn thought disdainfully. Both Trevor and the girl were wearing evening clothes, and she was hanging on to his arm for dear life. Robyn's gaze dropped to the legend below the photograph. It was written in typically breathless, movie mag style.

13

"Hot young star Deborah Hart steps out with best-selling author Trevor Barrone after shedding hubby No. 2. Will the dashing young adventurer be Hart-breaker No. 3?"

Robyn grimaced, uncertain whether she was most disgusted by the over-exposed curves of the actress, Trevor Barrone's movie star smile, or the ridiculous writing. She handed the clipping back. Mrs. Barrone looked at her expectantly.

"He's very handsome," Robyn finally said reluctantly.

"His father was too. And his grandfather as well," Mrs. Barrone said, smiling with fond memory. Then she sighed. "But the Barrone men have always had a wild streak. I just hope Trevor finds himself some nice, sensible young lady and settles down soon."

Glancing again at the clipping in Mrs. Barrone's hand, Robyn somehow doubted that Trevor Barrone was ever going to have much interest in some "nice, sensible young lady." His taste obviously ran more in the direction of lush curves and seductive eyes than sensible character.

"I can't help feeling Tim would be alive today if that — that woman hadn't led him astray," Mrs. Barrone murmured.

It was the only subject on which the elderly woman ever showed any bitterness. Her generous attitude toward her grandson's treatment of her, and her resigned attitude toward the "wild streak" in the Barrone men in general, did not extend to Trevor's mother. Robyn knew the story well.

Mrs. Barrone and her husband had come to Caverna Bay from Oklahoma soon after their marriage. Bill Barrone had logged in the redwood forests for years until an accident crippled him. Then he ran a gas station in town. They had only the one son, Tim. Tim went off to college, much to the wonder and pride of his parents, but there he fell in love with a young woman from well-to-do, southern California parents. She, in Mrs. Barrone's old-fashioned words, led Tim "astray." She liked action, excitement and money. Tim killed himself trying to keep her happy, according to Mrs. Barrone. Robyn wasn't sure that was exactly accurate, but it was true that Tim Barrone had died in some sort of yachting accident in the Caribbean, with rumors of wild parties and drug use.

Up until that time, Robyn gathered, the young wife's bad features had been at least partially redeemed by the fact that she had produced a grandson, Trevor. He often spent entire summers with his grandparents here in Caverna Bay while his parents flew off to France or Spain. All that ended when

Tim died. His young widow quickly remarried and that was practically the last Mrs. Barrone ever heard of her grandson.

Until about three years ago when Trevor Barrone suddenly became front-page news. He had turned up in Johannesburg, South Africa, with a harrowing tale of an almost incredible escape through the jungles of some small African country in the throes of revolution. He had been in the country on some sort of geological mineral survey but the revolutionaries had accused him of spying and imprisoned him in an underground cell with a death sentence hanging over his head. With the aid of a missionary's daughter he had somehow escaped, defying crocodiles, snakes, unfriendly natives and tropical disease.

The rest was "history," as the tabloids liked to say. Trevor wrote a book about his experiences. It became a best-seller, picked up awards and won praise from both critics and public. The movies had snapped it up, of course. The film was an even bigger success than the book. There was already talk of an Academy Award nomination.

Actually, at first Robyn was doubtful that the Trevor Barrone of the newspaper stories was really Mrs. Barrone's grandson, but Mrs. Barrone herself never had any doubt.

She religiously saved every word she could find about him, every clipping, every advertisement for the book or movie. They were all part of her scrapbook. A year or so ago, unknown to Robyn, she had written to him and actually received a reply, confirming that he really was her grandson. Since then the money and occasional extravagantly unsuitable gifts had arrived.

Now Mrs. Barrone flipped fondly through the scrapbook. It started with a handful of photographs taken during the summers Trevor visited, snapshots showing a dark-haired boy, vaguely arrogant looking even at the age of seven or eight, Robyn thought. From there the scrapbook skipped to the first newspaper pictures from Johannesburg, a rather blurred photograph showing a gaunt young man with a ragged beard and tattered clothing. There were more clippings, then the dust jacket from his book. The photograph on it showed just the head and shoulders, the beard neater but the handsome face still unsmilingly arrogant. And now there was this latest picture of a well dressed, sophisticated young man enjoying all the fruits of his success.

Robyn stood up. "Are you sure there isn't anything I can do?"

"You can hand me the roll of tape over

there on the television so I can fasten this clipping in the scrapbook," Mrs. Barrone suggested. She smiled. "Won't Trevor be surprised when he sees my scrapbook?"

Robyn bit her lip. "Mrs. Barrone, please — you mustn't be disappointed if —"

"He's coming," Mrs. Barrone said firmly. "Even when Trevor was only six years old, he never broke a promise. I could always count on him."

But six-year-olds didn't have a taste for fame and bright lights and voluptuous blondes, Robyn thought wryly. Aloud she said, "How old is Trevor now?"

Mrs. Barrone didn't have to calculate. "Thirty-one," she said promptly. "His birthday was in August. I remember a little birthday party I had for him one year, he was four years old . . ." Mrs. Barrone was off again on her favorite subject.

Usually Robyn didn't mind listening, knowing how dear the subject was to the elderly woman's heart, but this afternoon Robyn found the conversation uncomfortably grating. Damn Trevor Barrone, she thought suddenly, angrily. If he didn't show up after telling his grandmother he was coming, she personally was going to write or call and give him a piece of her mind.

". . . like you."

In her anger Robyn had missed what Mrs. Barrone was saying. She apologized.

"I was just saying that I hope when Trevor finally settles down and marries that it is to someone just like you," Mrs. Barrone said. She reached out a veined hand and squeezed Robyn's firm, tanned one. "I don't know what I'd have done without you these last few years. Your aunt was so good to me before she died and then you took up right where she left off. You're just like a granddaughter to me."

Robyn laughed and hugged the thin shoulders. "I need a grandmother just as much as you need a granddaughter, so it all works out even."

"And it's time you thought about marrying too," Mrs. Barrone chided, sharp blue eyes suddenly inspecting Robyn closely. "Why, when I was your age I was married and a mother already. What about you and that Larry fellow?"

Robyn shrugged. "We're just friends. I'm in no hurry."

Mrs. Barrone frowned disapprovingly but did not pursue the subject. "Will you stay and have some stew with me?" she invited.

Ordinarily Robyn would have stayed, perhaps mixing up some baking powder biscuits to go with the stew, but today she declined. Mrs. Barrone undoubtedly would want to keep on talking about her grandson, and Robyn was afraid if she heard much more she would come out with what she really thought of the man, that he was totally self-centered, completely materialistic, and obviously a woman chaser to boot. And, as far as Robyn was concerned, good looks and what the tabloids called a "charismatic personality" could never make up for those flaws.

"I'll run over after I get back from the beach tomorrow," Robyn promised.

She checked the simmering stew and added a little water before slipping into the oversized yellow slicker, a fisherman's discard, again. She tucked her long hair up under the floppy rain hat and waved to Mrs. Barrone from the front door.

It was one steep block down to the main street, then two blocks over to Robyn's little gift and curio shop. She went around back to her small but comfortable living quarters. Two children, oblivious to the storm, were playing in the park of giant redwoods nearby, clambering over the huge redwood stump with the walkway cut through it. Larry McAllister's car was just pulling into Robyn's narrow driveway.

He braked and called to Robyn. "Hey,

what're you doing out on foot on a day like this?"

Robyn approached the car. The back seat was full of framed paintings stacked together like so much cordwood.

"I like storms. Don't you know that by now?" Robyn said lightly.

Larry groaned and twisted his pleasant, freckled features into a grimace. "If you didn't look like a yellow angel in that crazy outfit, I'd come right out and say that was a dumb statement." He carelessly tossed a box of redwood pieces with forest scenes painted on them into the back seat and made room for Robyn. "C'mon, let's go down to Mama-Jo's and have a steak. I have to drive back down to 'Frisco tonight. I have an early appointment to unload some of this junk on a dealer there tomorrow."

"You shouldn't talk about your work that way," Robyn protested. "Just because you paint in quantity doesn't mean it isn't worthwhile. I'll bet your paintings have brought pleasure to more people than those of some big name artists."

"Don't you ever get tired of looking on the bright side of things?" he asked, grinning. "Sometimes I think your middle name must be Pollyanna."

Robyn flicked a wet sleeve at him, spray-

21

ing him with rainwater through the open window. He ducked and laughed. Theirs was a comfortable, easygoing relationship. Larry had finally quit asking her to marry him, though he still got a look in his eyes that bothered her sometimes. He painted for a living, and though his name was unknown and he'd never had a gallery showing in his life, he made a comfortable living supplying inexpensive seascapes and redwood scenes to tourist-oriented shops such as her own. He deprecated his own work and talent, but Robyn thought he was better than he gave himself credit for being.

Now he patted the seat again. "What do you say?"

Robyn shook her head. "Not tonight. I just turned down some of Mrs. Barrone's good stew so a steak can't tempt me either."

Larry sighed. "Still doing your good deed for the day I see, looking after the little old ladies of the world. Sometimes I think you really are too good to be true. But maybe that's why I love you."

He said the words lightly, but Robyn quickly changed the subject. "Mrs. Barrone had a letter from her grandson. She's all excited because he says he's coming to see her."

"The great author, Trevor Barrone himself? Right here in little old Caverna Bay? When?"

"He didn't say. I don't think he'll come at all myself, but . . ." She shrugged.

Larry gave her a long, thoughtful look. "You watch out for him if he does show up, you hear? If his pictures do him justice, he's a handsome rascal."

Robyn wrinkled her pert nose. "Ugh."

Larry laughed, then turned sober. "I really mean it, Robyn. You're sweet and naive —"

"You make me sound about ten years old!"

He ignored that. "And a whole lot prettier than you have any idea you are." Then he laughed again and put the car in gear. "But you'll probably be safe if you just keep that old yellow slicker on when he's around."

Robyn blew him a kiss and waved as he pulled away. "See you in a few days," she called. "I'll have the mobiles ready for your next trip down."

She went inside and fixed a grilled cheese sandwich and hot chocolate for supper. She put some good tapes on the stereo and settled down in her little workroom to work on the mobiles, her practiced eye selecting just the right bits and pieces of driftwood to make a pleasing, balanced construction.

Her mind kept drifting back to Trevor Barrone. Would he really show up here in

23

Caverna Bay? Unexpectedly the thought sent a little shiver through Robyn. She scoffed at it. He was handsome, of course. Almost too handsome, she decided critically. She had never been all that impressed with good looks anyway. Her experience had been that they were usually accompanied by an inflated ego. And there had certainly been nothing humble or modest about Trevor Barrone's description in the book of himself or the events in which he took part.

Of course the book was good, she had to admit grudgingly. She had taken Mrs. Barrone to Eureka to see the movie when it played there. That had proved a trifle embarrassing, since the movie was R-rated because of the violence and some sexy scenes. But Mrs. Barrone had never so much as blinked an eye or uttered a word of criticism. Robyn had liked the book a lot better than the movie. There really was a lot more to it than the sex and violence the movie had emphasized. But by the time he wrote the movie script Trevor had no doubt realized where the real money lay, Robyn thought cynically.

Robyn woke the next morning disappointed to hear water gurgling down the drainspout outside her bedroom window. She liked the storm but she had been looking

24

forward to going down to the beach this morning and picking up a fresh supply of interesting bits of driftwood. She loved the beach after a storm, loved stepping onto a virgin strip of freshly deposited sand. She always had the breathless feeling that maybe this time she was going to find something marvelous, an antique Oriental vase, perhaps. Maybe, deep down in some child-fantasy part of her, even a chest of Spanish gold. Of course, what she had found so far were just oddly shaped pieces of driftwood or maybe an unusual shell, but a few times there had been Japanese glass floats. And whatever she found, of course, eventually made its way into some article for the curio shop. Several times she had won awards for her creative constructions at various Beachcomber Festival exhibits.

Now she spent the morning working in a rather desultory fashion, going frequently to the window to check the state of the weather. By ten o'clock the rain had stopped and by noon the clouds were definitely breaking up. After lunch she slipped a hooded jacket over her jeans and T-shirt and headed for the trail that led over the slope separating the little town from the open Pacific. Tourists flocked to the beach on the bay but few of them even knew about this other beach. It was a series of beaches actually, the little crescents of sand separated by rocky ridges running out into the water. One in particular Robyn had always considered "her" beach. She felt the best driftwood always washed in there.

She crested the slope and paused to rest, disappointed to see that although the ocean had been generous with its deposit of fresh driftwood, most of it was in chunks and logs far too large to be useful to her. Some were still floating in the rough water, others rolling along the beach with the crash of the waves. She started down the steep trail anyway. The wind was still brisk but the sun, though a bit weak, had come out.

She was about halfway down the trail when she became aware of a disturbance out in the water. As she drew closer she could see that it was a seagull in some sort of difficulty and evidently weakening rapidly. Finally, walking along the edge of the surf, she got close enough to see what the problem was. Somehow the seagull had gotten entangled in some old fishing line. The poor thing was flopping helplessly, feet and one wing enmeshed. Part of the line was tangled in a half-submerged stump that wallowed with each movement of the water, dragging the terrified bird under.

Robyn paced back and forth, trying to

figure out what to do. She knew the dangerous unpredictability of any large object in the moving water, knew a wave could toss logs around as if they were toothpicks. The stump looked like a tentacled monster there in the surf, rising and falling as if it were alive. She shuddered to think what would happen if a wave rolled that monster over on her as she tried to free the bird. And yet she couldn't just leave the bird there, tangled and helpless. . . .

Quickly she jerked off her shoes and kicked them toward the silvered driftwood already lining the beach. She tossed her jacket after them, knowing she was going to need something dry to put on afterward. Determinedly she waded toward the rolling stump, feeling the pull of the water as it sucked the fine gravel from beneath her toes. The seagull flopped pathetically. The water surged back in, flooding around Robyn's thighs, then her waist. She fought down a feeling of panic as it drained away again, pulling at her.

She was almost at the stump now. She could see where the fishing line was wound around one of those tentacled roots. All she had to do was pull it free and then she could take the bird to a safe place on shore and untangle it there.

Another wave attacked her. She reached for the stump to steady herself but it rolled and weaved, sending her stumbling to keep out of its path. A wave rolled over her, drenching her from head to foot. The wind was blowing even harder than she had realized. She heard a cry, almost a human cry she thought for a moment, but then she decided it must be the terrified seagull.

She tried again. This time she got a hand on the fishing line but the root on which it was caught was on the far side of the stump. She yanked on the line, felt it bite into the smooth flesh of her hands, but it wouldn't break. The seagull floundered helplessly. Frantically Robyn tried to work her way around to the other side of the rolling stump. Then what she had dreaded happened. An oversized wave lifted the huge stump as if it were a toy.

Something hit her and flung her aside. But it wasn't the stump. Water washed over her and she came up choking and gasping as the stump rolled harmlessly on by her. She wiped her eyes, feeling the sting of salt. The water sloshed around her and she struggled to rise, but she had twisted her left knee when she fell and it wouldn't respond.

"What the hell do you think you're doing? Don't you know you could get killed trying a fool stunt like that? Didn't you hear me yell at you?"

Robyn brushed a tangle of hair away from her face and stared up at the man, realizing it was he who had flung her out of the path of the wave-tossed stump. Another wave sent her floundering in the sand and he towered over her.

He was tall, broad-shouldered in a blue windbreaker, denim levis molded to lean thighs. Thick, dark hair, wrap-around sunglasses, thin scar running along chiseled jawline, lips twisted in anger or disgust. Rivulets of water slid down the smooth nylon windbreaker. He evidently hadn't had time to take off his boots and they were soaked too. Robyn eyed him warily, oddly shaken, with the strange feeling that his harsh action in flinging her to safety could just as easily turn to hostile violence in different circumstances. There was a powerful, primitive vitality about him, a raw maleness that was disturbing in its intensity.

"Th— thank you," Robyn finally managed to say. "I didn't realize the surf was so heavy."

"You'd better get out of the water."

A floating branch jabbed Robyn in the ribs and he strode over and helped her roughly to her feet. She blinked back tears of pain as the sudden movement sent a jolt of pain through her twisted knee.

"Are you all right?" he asked sharply.

"Yes, I'm fine. The seagull —" She looked around. The oversized wave had thrust the stump far enough up on the sand that it was stuck. The bird was safe from the water now but still trapped and struggling feebly.

His gaze followed hers. "You mean you risked your life to save a damn seagull?"

Robyn hobbled toward the bird, favoring her injured leg. She knelt down, trying to untangle the snarled fishline, but by now her hands were too numb and stiff to do more than fumble with it uselessly.

He squatted beside her, watched for a moment, and then silently took over the job. She watched as he deftly unwound the tangled line from the seagull's feet, competently if not too patiently, cradling the bird under his arm while he worked. Finally only the wing remained caught. Robyn stared at it in dismay as she realized this portion of line was still attached to the stump.

"We need a knife!" she said. She knew the line wouldn't break. She had tried.

He didn't say anything. He wrapped the line around both hands, stretching it taut between them. Robyn watched as the fishline tightened and then cut cruelly into the tanned hands. His face showed no reaction and the pressure never faltered. She winced as the line cut deeper — and then snapped.

Quickly he unwound the line from the bird's wing and set the creature free. It wobbled off unsteadily but with all parts evidently still in working order. He tossed the fishline at her.

"Next time you'd better just accept the fact that nature is cruel or you'll wind up as badly off as the bird," he advised.

"Getting caught in fishline isn't 'nature,'" she retorted. "That's man's doing." She tucked the line in her pocket to discard at home so it couldn't endanger some other innocent creature.

He took the wrap-around sunglasses off and wiped them with a handkerchief. His eyes, Robyn noted, were an almost startling shade of deep, intense blue. Uneasily she watched him, feeling a vague sense of recognition. Yet he certainly wasn't a local. And she would have definitely remembered if he had done no more than wander casually into her gift shop.

"Tourists don't usually find this beach," she commented.

"That is exactly what I was thinking," he agreed.

He gave her an impersonal look of appraisal and Robyn was uncomfortably aware of her wet, shabby clothes, sand-covered feet, and hair plastered wetly to her head. Then, as his gaze dropped, she was even more uncomfortably aware of the wet T-shirt clinging to her breasts like a second skin. He replaced the concealing sunglasses, a gesture that struck Robyn as rather Hollywoodish since clouds had blotted out the sun again. She hobbled over to her old canvas shoes and sat on a log to put them on. She was chilled and shivering by the time she finally found her jacket where the wind had tossed it among the driftwood. She tried not to favor the injured knee, aware of the man's gaze on her and feeling his scorn for the way she had injured herself in concern over a mere bird. He disdainfully ignored his own dripping clothes and soaked boots.

"Can you make it back up the trail?" he asked.

"Yes, I think so."

There was a questioning tilt to his head, obvious in spite of the concealing sunglasses. She was perched on a log and made no move to start up the trail.

"I think I'll just sit here awhile and — and enjoy the scenery," Robyn said lamely. It was obviously a ridiculous statement since she was wet from head to toe, cold and shiv-

ering, and a light drizzle had started again. But somehow she didn't want to walk up the trail with him. She folded her arms, preparing to stay right there until he left, no matter how foolish she might look to him.

He shrugged, obviously not concerned if she chose to sit there cold and wet. But instead of starting up the trail himself he headed for the rocky point stretching out into the water.

"Where are you going?" she asked, puzzled.

"There's a cave carved in the rocks by the water on the other side of this point."

Robyn stared at him. "How did you know that?"

"I used to play there when I was a boy. Buried a treasure there one time. Four marbles and a pocket knife and a package of gum. Maybe I'll see if it's still there."

It was hard to imagine this rugged, arrogant man as a boy, dreamily burying boyish treasure in the sand. Suddenly a wave of apprehension washed over her. Dark hair, rugged build, scar on the jaw. She remembered a scene from a movie, a flashing knife in the hands of a prison guard . . .

"Who — who are you?" she faltered.

He pulled the sunglasses off again, h glance somehow mocking as he looked ba

at her. "Is this your private beach that you can demand identification?"

"No, of course not, I just wondered —"

"I'm Trev Barrone."

Chapter Two

Trev Barrone.

The name echoed in Robyn's mind and she stared at him, mentally comparing the man standing before her now with the pictures she had seen. Yes, it was Trevor Barrone, no doubt about that. She probably would have recognized him, she decided, except that in all the photographs he had been bearded and now he was clean-shaven. And the sunglasses, of course, had concealed his eyes with their unmistakable arrogance. Nor had the photographs revealed the incredible intensity of their blue coloring.

He raised a dark eyebrow. "The name seems familiar to you."

She refused to acknowledge that she had read his book, seen the movie, followed his name in the newspapers, if not with the devoted admiration of his grandmother, at least with curiosity. She tossed a windblown strand of hair out of her eyes. "Mrs. Barrone is a good friend of mine. She often speaks of you. She said you were coming, but —"

Robyn broke off. Her own opinion had been that Trevor Barrone would never show up, and obviously that was wrong because here he was before her. A little lamely she finished, "I just wasn't expecting you this soon. How long do you plan to stay?"

He turned his back to the wind, hunching his broad shoulders slightly. "I'm not sure yet. I need a few days of rest and relaxation. There are some places I want to see again, such as the old cave over there." He jerked his head toward the rocky ridge.

Guiltily Robyn realized that it was on account of her that he was standing there soaking wet. She was shivering but the only concession he made to wind and cold was that slight hunching of the shoulders. "I'm sorry you got wet helping me," Robyn apologized. "I really do appreciate the help. And I'm sure the seagull is even more appreciative."

"I took you to be a tourist who didn't know any better than to go wading around where you might get hurt. If you live here, you certainly should have known better." His voice was contemptuous in an impersonal sort of way.

Robyn was a little taken aback by his superior attitude. "I couldn't just let the poor bird suffer —"

He suddenly looked at her more closely, and Robyn was all too aware of how she must compare with the glamorous starlets he liked. She wore no makeup and the wind had dried the salt water on her face and tossed her hair in wild disarray.

"You wouldn't be the helpful little Robyn my grandmother is always talking about, would you?" he asked suddenly.

Helpful little Robyn. Furiously she realized he was ridiculing her. The slight softening she had felt toward him for actually showing up to visit his grandmother vanished. She drew herself up to her full height, which she realized with annoyance was not particularly impressive, since she still had to tilt her head back to meet his gaze. "I am Robyn Christopher," she stated icily.

"Then it appears that I am in your debt for being so helpful to my grandmother in so many ways," he stated with a polite nod of his head.

Somehow the gesture seemed more mocking than courteous. "I'm sure she would have appreciated a little helpfulness from a member of her family over the years too," she snapped. She hesitated, realizing suddenly she could be accusing him unfairly. "But I suppose you might not have known where she was since she had more or less lost contact with you."

"I knew," he said.

The flat, unemotional statement angered Robyn even more. She clutched the jacket around her. The wind was increasing, whipping drops of rain and surf around them. "Why have you come here?" she asked bluntly.

"I told you. Rest and relaxation —"

"According to the gossip columns you usually find more interesting ways to amuse yourself than visiting an elderly woman in a closed-up resort town!"

He looked down at her, and for a moment she thought he was simply going to tell her to mind her own business. Then he shrugged. "I plan to take my grandmother back down to southern California with me. I'm buying a house out near Palm Springs. The desert climate will be better for her arthritis, and I can see that she receives proper care there."

Robyn was surprised, not only by Trevor Barrone's plan but also by Mrs. Barrone's evident ready acceptance of it. She stepped back as the rising tide sent a surge of foam almost to her feet. "That's very considerate of you. I'll miss her." She hesitated. "To tell the truth, I'm a little surprised that she is willing to leave Caverna Bay. It's been her home for so many years."

He shrugged again. "I haven't told her about it yet."

"In other words, you're simply planning to *tell* her that you're moving her off to Palm Springs?" Robyn asked in disbelief.

"I think I know what is best," he said calmly.

He would make the decisions. *He* knew best. He was exactly what she expected after seeing those pictures of him: arrogant, supremely self-confident, high-handed.

But there was something else about him that she had not expected. Uneasily she tried to place exactly what it was. Actually, she decided critically, he wasn't as handsome as the photographs had made him out to be. His jaw was more angular, his face leaner, somehow harsher and more experienced looking, with tiny lines radiating from the corners of his eyes.

And yet, in spite of being less handsome, there was some other quality about him which the pictures had failed to show. Robyn was aware of it now as he stood there with legs spread and braced, the surf pounding behind him, the wind lifting his dark hair. There was a coiled readiness about him, like a predator poised to strike, a raw masculinity that had little to do with good looks or clothing. The thin scar along his chiseled jawline added to his harsh virility.

Unexpectedly Robyn shivered again, but this time the prickle of her skin had nothing to do with wind or cold. It came from within her, an unwilling reaction to Trevor Barrone as a man and she as a woman, a disturbing, primitive surge that she had never felt before.

She tried to scoff at her reaction. She had never been attracted to a man strictly on the basis of a sexual magnetism. She had also always had a certain scorn for macho, muscle types who paraded around flaunting their sex appeal.

But he wasn't really that type, she thought reluctantly. The book he had written was violent but brilliantly executed. The strong hands were perfectly groomed, the only flaw the red line left by the cruel bite of the fishline. The physique was powerful but lithe and lean, not muscle-bound. The clothing was conservative, no silk shirt deliberately open to the waist to flaunt a hairy chest.

No, Trevor Barrone needed none of those macho affectations. He didn't have to flaunt anything. That powerful aura of masculinity came from within, as much a part of him as his aloof self-assurance.

Determinedly Robyn shook off that unfamiliar, disturbing reaction within her. His personality was hardly as "charismatic" as the tabloids had described. Some female reporter had probably just been bowled over by all that rugged sex appeal, Robyn thought scornfully. What he projected was just Hollywood image stuff. He probably stood in front of a mirror and practiced that smouldering, intense look, she thought contemptuously.

His mouth moved in the suggestion of a humorless smile. She was embarrassed to realize he was well aware of her scrutiny and appraisal.

"Are you disappointed?" he asked dryly.

"I — I don't know what you mean," she faltered, startled.

He shrugged. "Sometimes people are disappointed when they meet me in person. They seem to expect the actor who played the Trevor Barrone role in the movie. An interviewer once asked if this had given me an identity problem."

"And has it?"

Again the negligent shrug. He might have been standing in some elegant drawing room instead of soaking wet on a storm-tossed beach. "As far as I'm concerned if there is any identity problem, the actor has it. I know who I am."

"I'm sure you do," Robyn murmured.

Fighter, adventurer, lover. She had a mental image of one of those vivid love scenes from the movie, and she was suddenly eager to be away from this man.

She stuck her hands in her jacket pockets and turned toward the trail, but she had momentarily forgotten the twisted knee. It buckled beneath her and she lurched toward him. His arms shot out, caught and steadied her as she regained her balance. Her body never touched his, but she was suddenly, almost electrically aware of his hard, lean strength. Their eyes met and her breath caught as that unfamiliar feeling jolted through her again. She jerked away, brushing windblown hair out of her eyes.

"I'm sorry," she said stiffly, struggling for composure. "I — I slipped in the sand."

"Perhaps I'll see you again before my grandmother and I are ready to leave," he suggested. There was an odd look in those intense, blue eyes, and Robyn suddenly remembered Larry's warning. She was no match for a glamorous starlet, but Robyn suspected Trevor Barrone could be harshly practical about settling for what was available.

"I don't think so," she said aloofly. "I'm very busy."

His eyebrows lifted. "Customers rushing

in and out of the gift shop?" he suggested dryly. "I believe I saw a sign on the door that read, 'Open Saturday and Sunday. Closed Weekdays.' "

It was true. During the slack winter season she opened the shop only on weekends. She flushed, realizing she had been neatly trapped, but she lifted her head defiantly. Trevor Barrone needn't think that just because she was a plain, small-town girl she would fall breathlessly into his best-seller arms. Abruptly she changed the subject.

"Don't you think having a grandmother around may — um — inhibit your life-style? Why do you really want to take her with you?"

He scowled. "Because she is my grandmother. Because that shack is no decent place to live and I can offer her better. Because I owe her —"

"And do you think that a fancy house, a bigger color television, hot and cold running maids, is really what she needs?" Robyn cut in, suddenly angry at his superior attitude. He thought he could ignore his grandmother for years and then step in and arbitrarily decide what was best for her. She was almost yelling now to be heard over the rising wind and the roar of the crashing waves.

"And what do you suggest?" he asked. He

barely raised his voice but it knifed clearly through the wind.

"I suggest what you give her is a little of yourself," Robyn shouted. She wasn't even aware of the rising tide swirling around her feet. "What she needs is *you*. Your love. Your attention. Some peace of mind. She worries about you. She doesn't need a lot of materialistic junk like you've been sending her. Does it ease your conscience to send her a television or a microwave oven she's scared to use? Do you think setting her up in a fancy house and then ignoring her will make her happy?"

"I intend to give her whatever she needs," he said coldly. He gave her another appraising glance with eyes that had turned to blue steel. With a curt nod he suddenly turned and started toward the rocky point again. Furiously Robyn refused to be dismissed simply because *he* had decided the conversation was over.

"Or perhaps what you're really after is the publicity and headlines," she called after him. " 'Best-Selling Author Rescues Grandmother From Poverty.' I'm surprised you didn't have a reporter around to record your heroic plunge to save me from the man-eating stump . . ."

Robyn's voice trailed off as she realized she

had gone too far. The thin scar stood out in a white line along the angry set of his jaw, and the eyes were dark with fury. She took a wary step backward, suddenly aware that Trevor Barrone was not like the tame, safe men she had always known. She shivered violently, though he, as wet as she, stood there impassively ignoring the wind and rain.

This was a ridiculous conversation, she decided abruptly. Ridiculous and pointless since Trevor Barrone obviously had ice in his veins instead of blood. He was the kind of man who thought any woman could be bought, even a grandmother.

"I promised your grandmother I'd be over today. Would you please tell her I won't be able to make it?" Robyn said with all the dignity she could muster.

He gave a jerk of his head that might or might not have signified agreement, and Robyn turned and fled. This time she was careful to favor one leg enough to keep from stumbling. She gritted her teeth against the pain as she labored up the steep trail. When she glanced back, he was still watching her. Probably hoping she'd fall flat on her face, she thought furiously. Determinedly she struggled on, and the next time she surreptitiously glanced back he was just disappearing over the rocky point into the next shallow cove, unmindful of weather or wet clothing as he leaped over the spray-slickened rocks.

Serve him right if he caught pneumonia, Robyn sniffed as she paused to rest. Then, guiltily, she remembered he had gotten drenched helping her. It really had been a rather foolish, dangerous thing she had done, trying to rescue the bird with the stump jostling around in the water, she admitted to herself. Only last summer a man had been killed by a wave-tossed log a few miles north of the bay. Trev's scorn might have been justified.

But then, she thought, feeling vaguely puzzled, what he had done could be considered just as foolish and dangerous. He might not actually have saved her life, but he had certainly risked his own. She shrugged off the thought. His action probably had more to do with overblown male ego than real concern. She would probably read some melodramatic version of the incident in his next book.

Robyn was afraid the twisted knee might really be injured, but by the time she got home, took a couple of aspirins and settled in a hot tub, she felt only an occasional twinge of pain. Soaking there in the soothing, scented bubbles, she decided simply to ignore Trev Barrone while he was in town. She would just stay away from Mrs. Barrone's house too. The elderly woman wouldn't need her anyway while Trev was around. Of course, if Mrs. Barrone actually moved away, Robyn would have to go and say good-bye, but perhaps she could somehow avoid the man even then.

But deciding to avoid him did not necessarily mean she could keep him out of her mind, she found. Several times she saw him drive by the gift shop in his sleek Ferrari, sometimes alone, sometimes with Mrs. Barrone sitting proudly beside him. Even Larry, when he came by, had some comments to make about having seen Trevor Barrone taking his grandmother out to dinner, and how she had looked like a glowing girl out with her best beau. He tentatively inquired if Robyn had met Trevor yet. She replied carelessly that she had accidentally run into him on the beach.

"Not impressed?" Larry questioned lightly.

"I hardly think I'm going to impress him after those overdeveloped starlets he's usually seen with," Robyn said scornfully.

"Actually, I was thinking of the other way around. Of how he impressed you," Larry said slowly. He gave her a thoughtful look. "And I'd say he must have made quite an impression."

That wasn't true, Robyn thought as she unlocked the front door of the gift shop on Saturday morning. She had disliked Trevor Barrone before she met him and she disliked him even more now. If he had made an impression on her, it was only a negative one. He was insufferably arrogant, cold-blooded, materialistic and even a little frightening.

And yet, reluctantly, she had to admit she was more aware of him as a *man* than she had ever been of any other man. Generally her relationships with men were pleasant and uncomplicated, affectionate rather than passionate. She had always been a little scornful of people who let physical attraction blur their good sense.

But she had only to remember that almost electric jolt when Trev caught her in his arms, the shivery intensity of his blue eyes, to realize how powerful a force that sort of attraction could be. It angered her that he had aroused that unfamiliar, disturbing feeling within her. She didn't know the man. She didn't want to know him. She didn't even like him. . . .

Her thoughts broke off as she realized that the object of them was standing right there in the doorway to her small shop. The bell attached to the door jangled as he let the door slip shut behind him. Flustered, she flicked the feather duster over a row of knickknacks.

He was wearing tan slacks and a suede jacket. All he needed was a pipe to complete the studied air of rustic elegance suitable for a best-selling author on vacation, Robyn thought scornfully, trying to ignore how attractive he really did look.

She was suddenly, unexplainably, glad she was wearing the new rust-colored pantsuit she had picked up in Eureka a few weeks ago. It wasn't elaborate but it was stylish and emphasized her slim waist. She was glad, too, that she'd touched up her eyes with smoky eyeshadow and brightened her mouth with a coppery lipstick. At least she didn't look like some poor little waif washed in by the tide this time.

Then she was annoyed with herself. What did she care how she looked to him?

"How is your knee?" he asked finally.

"Fine, thank you," she said warily, recalling their last meeting had not exactly ended on the best of terms.

"My grandmother has tried to call you several times. You didn't answer."

Robyn dusted the glass jewelry case, guiltily avoiding his eyes. Ignoring a ringing phone was not something she usually did, but it had seemed better than making excuses to Mrs. Barrone to avoid meeting Trev again. She wondered if he had told his grandmother about their stormy encounter on the beach.

Now Robyn said evasively, "Perhaps I was out. I go to the beach quite often."

He wandered around, inspected her driftwood mobiles, fingered one of the comic animals she had created from bits of driftwood and shells, looked without interest at the rows of inexpensive trinkets and souvenirs she bought from a dealer. His virile presence dominated the small room, but he seemed restless and uncharacteristically ill at ease. She kept wondering why he was here. Trevor Barrone hardly seemed the type to make social calls on poor little shopgirls.

"Have you been enjoying your vacation?" she asked, her voice neutrally polite.

"The area has changed a lot since I was here as a boy. There was no development at all along the south side of the bay then. There are some beautiful homes there now."

Robyn murmured something noncommittal. The people on that side of the bay were in a world apart from hers. Most of the places were summer homes belonging to physicians or lawyers from the San Francisco Bay area who had little to do with Caverna Bay's permanent residents. There were rumors that the newest house in that exclusive area, a soaring structure of redwood and glass and stone built on an outcropping overlooking the entire bay, belonged to a well-known television personality.

Trev stared into the glass jewelry case.

"Will you have another book coming out soon?" she asked. He didn't seem inclined to make small talk but the silent void made her uneasy.

"Not in the immediate future." He paused. "Actually, I don't really think of myself as a writer. I'm a geologist. I'm in the process of forming my own mineral exploration company."

"Perhaps you'll be fortunate enough to have some more noteworthy experiences," Robyn murmured.

"I'll be sure to take a photographer along to document my experiences this time," he agreed sardonically.

Robyn flushed, knowing he was referring to her uncalled-for remark on the beach about his having a reporter there to record his heroic gesture in helping her. "I'm sorry for what I said." She dusted the cash register and straightened a box of whimsical gift labels. "I read your book. It was really very interesting."

"Thank you."

"It's hard to believe such brutality and in-justice are really happening today."

"Everything in the book is true, exactly as it happened," he said harshly.

Robyn shuddered as she remembered his vivid account of the attack on his life by the prison guard. The thin scar seemed less obvious today, but it would always be there, a brutal reminder that in some parts of the world the man with a knife or gun could be accuser, judge and executioner.

The door opened and a middle-aged couple came in. The man looked bored but the woman rushed around gushing enthusiastically about Robyn's creations and Larry's paintings. She finally selected one of the more elaborate driftwood mobiles. As Robyn was giftwrapping it, she noticed a paperback book sticking out of the woman's large purse. It was Trev's book. Robyn wondered what the woman would think if she knew she was in the presence of the author, but somehow Robyn knew Trev was in no mood for signing autographs.

The couple left, the man muttering about the miserable weather. Trev, who had been looking out the window with his back to them, returned to the counter.

"Do you know whatever became of the missionary's daughter who first helped you escape?" Robyn asked curiously.

Trev shook his head. "Look, if you don't mind, I'd really rather not talk about all that. It's a time of my life I'd like to forget."

The sharp words stung. "I didn't mean to pry," Robyn said stiffly. He made no reply and Robyn felt her anger rising. More than likely his lack of interest in the discussion was because he wasn't getting paid for it this time. "Writing a best-seller seems a rather odd way to try to *forget* something," she remarked tartly.

"I wrote the book as something of a — a catharsis," he said. "I couldn't get some of what had happened out of my head. I had nightmares about it. Someone suggested that it might help if I put it all down on paper. At the time I wasn't even thinking about publication." He sounded as if he made the admission almost reluctantly. Then his chiseled lips twisted grimly. "But it seems the public has a taste for blood and violence."

"And sex," she murmured.

Unexpectedly he laughed. "Unfortunately I didn't have as much control over the movie script as I would have liked. Some of the people I dealt with in the movie world could make a cookbook about yogurt seem sexy." The laughter died abruptly as he eyed her with those intense blue eyes and his voice was almost brutal when he added, "But I'm not trying to say I was some kind of saint either. It was another world," he finished abruptly. "As I said, I'd rather forget it. You make these?" His tanned hand touched one of the airy driftwood creations.

Robyn looked up, startled at the sudden change of subject. But from the scowl on his face she suddenly realized he really would rather not talk about those events from the past. She found the realization disconcerting. She had suspected he was the kind of man who delighted in going over the gory details again and again, glorying over his own heroics.

"Yes. I make them mostly out of things I find on the beach," she said, uncertain whether or not he was really interested.

"And the seascapes?"

"A friend of mine paints those. He does some redwood scenes on black velvet that are quite striking and very popular."

"Boyfriend?" he asked unexpectedly.

"No." She hesitated. "Just a friend."

He wandered around again, still restless, as if he found the small shop too confining. Intuitively, Robyn knew he had some specific reason for coming here and she wondered why it was taking him so long to get around to it.

"How long have you lived here?" he asked.

"About four years. My aunt owned the shop when I came. She died last year and left it to me."

He lightly fingered a display of handmade agate earrings on the counter. "And what brought you here in the first place? It seems a little on the dull side for a pretty young girl."

Pretty young girl. He made her sound like a child in rompers. "It's not dull during the summer season," she said defensively. "And besides, I like the quiet beaches and the redwoods and the storms. I'm afraid I wouldn't care for the kind of life you're accustomed to."

He allowed himself a trace of a smile. "You didn't answer my question."

"I came after I finished high school, intending to work for my aunt just for a summer season," she answered briefly. "She fell ill and I — I didn't feel I could leave her."

"So now you're looking after my grandmother. And rescuing seagulls in distress." His voice sounded mocking.

"I'm sorry if you find that amusing or boring," Robyn said stiffly. "Actually, Mrs. Barrone has done a great deal for me too. She's been all the family I've had the past year."

He was standing by the window again. She studied him out of the corner of her eye as she unnecessarily rearranged some of Larry's miniature redwood paintings. He looked sauve and sophisticated standing there, and yet that aura of raw strength and almost primitive masculinity was just beneath the surface.

But his voice was politely civilized when he said, "Parents?"

She looked at him blankly, realizing she had lost the thread of the conversation.

"You said my grandmother was your only family," he prompted. "What about your parents?"

"They were killed in an auto accident shortly after I came here to Caverna Bay."

"I'm sorry." He sounded sympathetic and she remembered that he had lost his father too, and at a much earlier age than she had. Quickly she quashed an unwanted twinge of sympathy.

"Mr. Barrone —," she began crisply.

"Call me Trev," he suggested with the trace of a smile. "Considering that we're practically family."

Robyn thought she detected a note of irony in his voice and she ignored the suggestion. "Mr. Barrone, I don't think you came over here just to inquire about my

56

knee. And you've made it plain you don't care to discuss your book. So why *have* you come?"

"Actually —" He broke off and hesitated. "Actually, I came to ask a favor of you."

Obviously, asking favors did not come easily to Trev Barrone, considering how long it had taken him to get around to it. A muscle under the thin scar jerked spasmodically. No doubt he considered having to ask for help a weakness, Robyn thought wryly. A tart comment rose to her lips but she bit it back, curious about what he could possibly want of her. She waited, her expression guarded.

"As you know," he began, "my plan is to take my grandmother back to Palm Springs with me."

Robyn nodded.

"She doesn't want to go." He sounded slightly indignant. Almost angrily he added, "I would appreciate it if you would try to talk some sense into her. She respects your opinion. I think she would listen to you."

Robyn was uncertain whether his anger was directed at his grandmother's stubbornness or at Robyn herself because he had been forced to come to her for help.

"Perhaps if you showed her a picture of the new house —," Robyn began.

"Don't be facetious," he growled. "I realize you expressed a certain — lack of enthusiasm for my plan to move her, but I'm sure if you consider the advantages, you will realize it really is best for her."

"Has she said why she doesn't want to go?" Robyn asked finally.

Trev shrugged. "She says she's lived here most of her life and likes it. She says she's too old to move to some strange place."

"I'm sure making such a drastic change could be difficult for an older person," Robyn murmured.

"Will you talk to her?" he asked.

"But if she really doesn't *want* to go —," Robyn began slowly.

"Good Lord, look at the advantages," he said, sounding exasperated. "The hot, dry climate will be better for her than all this damp cold. I can be sure she'll receive any medical care she needs. She'll have the best of food, a nice place to live, everything she hasn't had all these years. She can raise all the damn plants she wants."

"She could keep her little place here and just come to visit you now and then."

He looked at her, the chiseled lips suddenly hardening. "Be honest with yourself," he said harshly. "Are you really thinking about what is best for *her?*"

"Of course I am," Robyn retorted heatedly. "She has her friends here . . ."

Her voice trailed off under his probing gaze. Was she, she wondered uncomfortably, really thinking about what was best for Mrs. Barrone? Or was she letting her unwillingness to help Trevor Barrone in his arrogant decision blind her to the very real advantages of the plan?

As he pointed out, Mrs. Barrone would undoubtedly have the best of care, and the climate might indeed be beneficial. Robyn usually looked in on Mrs. Barrone twice a week during the busy summer season and at least every other day during the winter. But Mrs. Barrone could easily fall sick or injured and lie there helpless and unattended until it was too late. Yet Robyn knew how she would feel if someone tried to yank her away from the home she had always known, even if the move would be best for her. But perhaps, Robyn thought guiltily, she was being a little selfish because she would miss the dear old lady so much.

"It would take a lot of the burden off you," Trev pointed out. "Surely a pretty girl like you has better things to do than look after someone else's garrulous old grandmother."

"I have never considered my friendship with Mrs. Barrone a burden!" Robyn gasped indignantly. "And if your opinion of her is a 'garrulous old grandmother,' it is no wonder she doesn't want to go with you!"

"I didn't mean that the way it sounded," Trev said, his voice gruffly apologetic. "I just want what is best for her."

"Maybe you should give more consideration to what she wants then," Robyn snapped.

"What she seems to want most," Trev said grimly, "is to see me safely married and settled down with some nice, sensible girl in some nice, sensible house. No doubt with nice, sensible children and a dog to match." He sounded thoroughly exasperated now.

"And you, I take it, have no intention of settling down with any nice, sensible girl," Robyn remarked.

But behind the tartness she was stifling laughter. She could just imagine Mrs. Barrone wagging a finger at him and urging him to settle down with some nice, sensible — interpret that *plain* — girl. And Trev Barrone's frustration with his grandmother's attitude was obvious. He just might have met his match in his grandmother, Robyn thought with a certain degree of satisfaction.

"You think it's funny, don't you?" he growled, almost glowering at her. When she managed a noncommittal shrug, his lips finally twitched in amusement too. "Well, I suppose it is in a way."

"Not really," Robyn finally managed to say, curbing her inward laughter. "She really does love you, you know, and she's just concerned and worried about you."

"I'm concerned about her too, but I'll pick my own wife, thank you."

Robyn wondered briefly if that meant he had already chosen one of the shapely starlets, but she did not pursue the subject. All that was really important was what was best for Mrs. Barrone. It was no concern of Robyn's whom, or even if, Trevor Barrone ever married.

"You will talk to her then?" Trev prodded again.

Robyn busied herself straightening jewelry inside the glass case. "I'll think about it," she said noncommittally.

Trev gave her a curt nod, obviously none too pleased with her attitude. He strode out of the small shop, the little bell jangling more than usual from the way he closed the door with ill concealed annoyance. She watched him slide into the Ferrari and slam the door shut. It was obvious, she thought wryly, that Trevor Barrone was not accustomed to getting an "I'll think about it" sort of answer from any request he made to a female. Of course, if he had made a request of some other kind . . .

Robyn jerked her mind away from that oddly tantalizing thought. Trev had called her "pretty" at least twice, but both times with that mocking inflection that somehow made the word sound disparaging rather than complimentary. "Pretty" wasn't enough for him, of course. It was in the same class as "nice" and "sensible." What he liked, she thought grimly, was a voluptuous, lush sort of beauty. And yet she knew she wasn't the only one who had felt that electric jolt when he caught her there on the beach. . . .

Well, he would be out of her life in a few days anyway, she thought firmly. Actually, her mind was already made up about persuading Mrs. Barrone to make the move. At Mrs. Barrone's age, the primary concern must be the availability of prompt, competent medical attention. In addition she would have good food and care and security. Even if Trev didn't pay as much attention to her as he should, Mrs. Barrone was bound to see more of him than she ever would here. Robyn was fairly confident she could persuade Mrs. Barrone to go.

But Robyn perversely decided she wasn't going to talk to Mrs. Barrone for a few days yet. Let Trev stew for a while. He expected every woman he encountered to jump at his every wish and she had no intention of being that accommodating.

She determinedly waited four full days before starting up the steep street toward Mrs. Barrone's house. It was after dark and another storm had blown in. Wind and rain whipped around Robyn's slim figure, but she wasn't wearing the shapeless yellow slicker and floppy rain hat this time. She had told herself as she slipped into a trim, belted jacket and flatteringly fashionable boots that she was dressing more attractively only because she really ought, as a young businesswoman, to pay more attention to her appearance. But deep down she knew that wasn't the real reason.

She felt vaguely let down when she realized the sleek Ferrari was not parked outside the little house. Perhaps Trev had taken his grandmother out to dinner again. No, the television set was on and there was a glimmer of light from inside.

She tapped on the door and called, "Are you in there, Mrs. Barrone?" She pushed the door open without waiting for an answer, as was her usual habit.

She gasped unbelievingly. A fallen lamp lay on its side, the angled light throwing garish shadows across the room. The television picture rolled, completely out of focus, as the voices chattered on. Wind and rain blew through the shattered window.

And Mrs. Barrone, her frail body almost lost in the tangled debris of overturned chair, broken pots and tangled plants, lay face down on the floor.

Chapter Three

Robyn rushed to the motionless figure, heart thudding with fear and apprehension. The frail hand felt cold and Robyn's own slim hands trembled as she searched for a pulse. Was it there? No — yes, maybe just the very weakest thread of life. Robyn yanked a shabby blanket off the even shabbier sofa and tucked it around Mrs. Barrone's limp body, shuddering at the unnatural twist of her right leg.

Rain whipped through the shattered window but that would have to wait. Robyn searched frantically for the phone, following the trailing cord until she found the phone near the fallen lamp, not more than a few feet from Mrs. Barrone's outstretched hand.

The emergency numbers were taped right to the receiver. Robyn had put them there herself. A lot of good they had done, she thought bitterly. She dialed, waited impatiently, willing someone to answer. Caverna Bay had neither doctor nor hospital, only a combination volunteer fire department and one-vehicle ambulance service. She kept her eyes fastened on the slight figure under the blanket, so motionless, so lifeless.

Finally the man on duty answered, his manner changing instantly as he realized the call wasn't just a social suggestion that the guys get together at the firehouse and play cards. Robyn knew it would take the ambulance several minutes to reach the house even though the station was only a few blocks away. She ran back to Mrs. Barrone and added another blanket to keep her warm. The stove was going full blast, but it was no match for the chill, wet air blowing through the window. Robyn found more blankets in the bedroom and stuffed them in the gaping hole, shutting off at least some of the draft.

Then she looked around slowly. It wasn't difficult to figure out what had happened. Mrs. Barrone had climbed on a chair and attempted to move one of the hanging plants. The pot had been too heavy for her, or she had simply slipped, sending the pot smashing through the window and crashing to the floor herself, dragging more pots with her.

It's all my fault, Robyn thought remorsefully, with an agonizing rush of guilt. She always moved the plants around for Mrs. Barrone. But since Robyn was avoiding her, Mrs. Barrone had obviously tried to do it herself. All because I was being stubborn,

Robyn berated herself, determined I was going to show Trev I wouldn't jump at his every request like —

Her thoughts broke off abruptly. She had been so shocked and frightened finding Mrs. Barrone like this that she hadn't even thought about Trev. But now that she was thinking about him, just where was he anyway? Where was the mighty best-selling author with all his alleged concern for his grandmother?

Robyn marched angrily toward the other small bedroom to see if his things were still there, not caring if he objected to the invasion of privacy. If he had simply picked up and abandoned —

Robyn's thoughts were interrupted by the wail of the ambulance siren and she changed direction and raced for the door. She held it open as the two men carried a stretcher inside. They nodded recognition at Robyn.

"What happened?"

It seemed easier not to go into involved explanations. "I don't know," Robyn said crisply. "I found her like this. I don't know how long she's been here."

The man knelt, felt Mrs. Barrone's wrist, then her thin throat. He nodded. "She's alive. But just barely."

An almost inaudible sigh escaped Mrs. Barrone's colorless lips as the men slipped her slight body onto the stretcher, but her eyes did not open. Robyn made the abrupt decision that she would ride in the ambulance. It would take too long to run home and get her own car. She didn't even think how she would get back after they reached the small community hospital at Redwood Valley.

The men sat up front and Robyn rode in back with Mrs. Barrone, holding tight to her hand although she knew the elderly woman was aware of nothing. The ride seemed endless, and Robyn found herself shivering in spite of the warmth of the vehicle and her own jacket. She tucked the blankets more closely around Mrs. Barrone's thin shoulders. There was a gash on her forehead, dried blood around it. How long had she lain there? Oh Lord, how long?

Robyn berated herself, thinking it was all her fault. If only she hadn't been so stubborn, hadn't let her dislike of Trevor Barrone keep her away from his grandmother. Mrs. Barrone depended on her, needed her. She should have come to Mrs. Barrone as soon as Trev had asked her to. Mrs. Barrone could right now be on her way to a marvelous new home in Palm Springs instead of lying here like this. And where, where was Trev? Had he simply abandoned his plan to move his grandmother, shrugged his shoulders at her stubbornness and walked away?

No, that wasn't like Trev, Robyn thought. Not that she was completely convinced of his great concern for his grandmother, but he was far too arrogant and determined simply to give in to an elderly woman's stubbornness. So what had happened? Important call from a big publisher or producer? Or some more personal request from one of the overdeveloped starlets? Whatever it was, Robyn decided grimly that she intended to give him a piece of her mind, and in something less than ladylike terms.

The ambulance pulled into the emergency entrance of the small, one-story hospital. Robyn hovered alongside as the stretcher was carried inside. A nurse rose quickly from behind a cluttered desk and a moment later a doctor appeared. Robyn followed him down the hallway, telling him what she knew, realizing she was almost babbling but somehow unable to stop. Here, in the bright lights, Mrs. Barrone looked even worse, her complexion gray, the features gaunt, the cut on her head a garish line.

Outside another brilliantly lit room the doctor stopped Robyn, gently but firmly telling her the nurse at the desk would need to get some information from her. Robyn obediently went back to the desk and automatically answered questions. Patient's name? Rose Barrone. Address? 120 Mill Street, Caverna Bay. Yes, Mrs. Barrone was covered under Medicare. No, Robyn wasn't a relative, just a friend. She gave Trev's name as next of kin. And where could Trevor Barrone be reached?

Robyn shook her head. "I don't know. He's been out of town." She spotted a pay phone on the far wall. "I'll try to call him."

Robyn deposited coins and gave the operator Mrs. Barrone's home phone number. She had no real expectation Trev would be there, but she didn't know where else to try to reach him. With astonishment she heard his terse "Hello?" after the first ring.

Robyn briefly explained what had happened and where they were. She held her anger back, realizing anything she said could be heard by the nurse at the desk, but storing the words up for later. Trev asked directions, said he'd be there as soon as possible and hung up without even saying good-bye.

Robyn sat on a vinyl couch, but she couldn't stay there for long. She stood up and paced the room restlessly. What was that odor that made all hospitals smell alike? she wondered vaguely. She jumped when the phone rang. The nurse answered it, checked some forms on her desk and hung up.

Robyn sat again, paced again. Angry dialogues with Trev raced through her mind. She felt slightly nauseated. There was something about those pale green walls, the glaring light and the pervasive hospital odor. She tried not to think of Mrs. Barrone as she had found her, so bloodless, so lifeless, but it was all she could think of. She riffled unseeingly through a year-old magazine. The nurse offered coffee. Robyn declined. She was standing with her back to the door, reading a sign about welfare patients, when the door burst open and Trev strode in.

Robyn's angry remarks, honed to a fine cutting edge while she waited for Trev, died on her lips. Instead she felt a sense of relief wash over her. His broad shoulders looked strong and capable, his jaw determined. She leaned weakly against the pale green wall, feeling drained, as if Trev's mere presence had taken an awful burden from her shoulders.

"Where is she?" he demanded without preliminaries. He was wearing dark slacks and jacket over a lighter colored turtleneck shirt, his dark hair beaded with droplets of rain.

"The doctor is with her —"

He strode past Robyn to the nurse. "What is Mrs. Barrone's condition?"

The cool, poised nurse looked at Trev as if she were about to put him in his place, but she evidently thought better of it and disappeared down the hallway. Robyn knew the nurse would never have responded to an inquiry from her in such a manner. She suddenly felt a surge of hope where she had felt only despair before. Trev would see that something was done. He would *make* something happen. He stood by the desk, a scowl on his face, but with an air of strength, authority and self-assurance. Robyn felt the strangest urge to melt against that secure strength, to find shelter in those powerful arms, to lean against him and let the held-back tears of fear and worry flow.

Then she caught herself abruptly and met his glance with a lift of her head. He might look strong and invincible, she thought scornfully, but where had he been when Mrs. Barrone needed him?

Trev hesitated a moment, then walked over to Robyn. "When did this happen?" he asked.

"I don't know. I called an ambulance as soon as I found her. I guess that was —" Robyn hesitated, forehead wrinkling. She seemed to have lost all sense of time. "Perhaps a couple of hours ago. She was evidently trying to move some of her hanging plants closer to the window and fell."

He raised a dark eyebrow. "I take it this was the first time you had visited her since our discussion in your shop."

"Yes. I was going over to talk to her about your plan to move her to Palm Springs. I've been — busy," Robyn added lamely by way of explanation for not going sooner.

"I see." The words were flat, expressionless, and yet somehow managed to convey utter contempt. He walked back to the desk, impatiently looking for the nurse.

"I'd have gone over sooner if I'd realized you weren't going to be there," Robyn said defensively.

"You were avoiding me?" The question was dry, accompanied by the quick lift of an eyebrow. He seemed to find the thought that she might have been avoiding him more curious than disturbing.

"I was under the impression that since you were with Mrs. Barrone I wouldn't be needed. I didn't realize you were going to walk out and abandon her." Robyn met his eyes defiantly, refusing to soften her accusation.

"I had to go out of town on business," he

said curtly, making plain he felt under no obligation to offer her any further explanation. "I tried to call you before I left but didn't get any answer. My grandmother assured me she would be fine and would get in touch with you herself."

"Then the accident could have happened shortly after you left because I never heard from her. How — how long have you been gone?" Robyn faltered.

"Almost three days."

Three days. Robyn felt the blood drain from her face. For three days poor Mrs. Barrone might have been lying there helpless. What chance could she possibly have after such an ordeal?

The nurse returned and spoke directly to Trev. "They've moved Mrs. Barrone into the intensive care unit. The doctor will be out to talk to you in a few minutes."

Trev leaned strong knuckles on the nurse's desk. "Look, I want the best of everything for her. If she needs a specialist, I'll have one flown in. And unless this hospital is better equipped than I think it is, you'd better get her ready for transfer to San Francisco."

The nurse looked affronted. "Really, Mr. Barrone, I can assure you —"

"I don't want assurances," he said grimly. "I want action."

He turned his back on the nurse, dismissing her. She looked nonplussed. Robyn knew the feeling. She quaked as he eyed her with the same harsh expression, but suddenly she was coldly furious. Here he was acting so superior, demanding the best for his grandmother after having given far less than the best of himself.

"How nice," she said sarcastically, not even bothering to lower her voice so the nurse wouldn't hear. "You want the 'best of everything' for her. Where were you all the years she needed you? Why didn't you do something for her when she was alive and well and could appreciate it?"

"I've tried, during the last year —"

"Oh sure, I know — the stove, the television, the microwave oven. Don't you know she doesn't care about those things? Have you seen her scrapbook? It doesn't have pictures of *things* in it. It's all about *you*."

"Please, miss, this is a hospital!" the nurse interjected, and Robyn suddenly realized her voice had risen shrilly. Trev just stood there impassively, his face expressionless.

Robyn lowered her voice, but she wasn't through yet. "Do you really think you can make up for all the years you neglected her by playing the big man and going around ordering the best of everything for her now?

75

Do you really think a fine, fancy funeral is going to mean anything to her?"

"She's that bad?" he asked narrowly.

"I — I don't know," Robyn faltered. The burst of anger had drained her, and, guiltily, she knew the anger was directed as much at herself as at Trev Barrone. If only she had gone to see the elderly woman sooner. . . .

They both looked up as a young, sandy-haired doctor walked in from the hallway. He was the same one Robyn had babbled to earlier. The nurse handed him some papers to sign. "You're Mrs. Barrone's relatives?" he inquired.

"I'm Trev Barrone, her grandson." Trev motioned toward Robyn. "This is Miss Christopher, a friend."

"Dr. Helgeson."

They all shook hands. Robyn felt on the verge of hysteria. Here they were, all being so civilized and polite, and Mrs. Barrone was in there dying.

"As the nurse has probably informed you, we've moved Mrs. Barrone into the intensive care unit. She's suffering from shock and her vital signs are very weak. Her right hip is broken, but in her present condition surgery is out of the question. She has cuts and numerous bruises. I think it is likely her fall resulted from a stroke."

"Is she going to live?" Trev asked bluntly.

"The prognosis is doubtful," the doctor said carefully.

Robyn pressed her lips together. It was what she had expected, and yet hearing the doctor say it hit her hard. She darted a glance at Trev. His face seemed impassive at first, and then she noted the little muscle jerking along his jawline. In spite of her anger, the almost imperceptible movement touched her. Perhaps he wasn't pure ice and stone.

"There's nothing that can be done?" Trev asked, his harsh voice immediately belying that touch of emotion Robyn thought she had detected in him.

"I wouldn't say that —"

"Specialists? Moving her to another hospital?"

The doctor did not seem as affronted by the suggestion as the nurse had been. "I'm waiting for a call from a colleague, Dr. Martin, now. I'm afraid moving her is, at the moment, out of the question."

"I see. Very well. As I told the nurse, if there's anything she needs, anything at all —"

"She'll have the best of care, Mr. Barrone."

Robyn knew there was an unspoken *but* on the end of that statement. *But it may not be enough.* The doctor turned and disappeared down the hallway. Trev turned to Robyn.

"Did you drive your car?" he asked.

"No, I rode in the ambulance."

"I'll take you home then." It was a statement, not an inquiry as to whether or not she wanted to go home. He took her elbow, firmly turning her toward the door.

Robyn jerked away. "I'm not leaving. How can you possibly think I could just go home when your grandmother —"

"There's nothing you can do for her."

"And what can you do for her?" Robyn retorted. "What good is a fancy home in Palm Springs now that she's dying? You think money can make anything right, but it can't. It's too late now to do anything."

"Robyn, what is past is over and done with," Trev said harshly. "And your continued harping on my mistakes can't help any of us. Now I'm taking you home."

"No," Robyn said flatly. She swallowed. "I — I'm sorry I'm yelling at you. I'm upset. I should have gone to see her earlier. Then she wouldn't have tried to move the plants herself and none of this would have happened."

Trev's harsh expression softened slightly. "Maybe what we both need is a cup of coffee."

Robyn and Trev walked down the quiet corridor. The hospital did not seem to be crowded or busy. They found the cafeteria. Coffee at this hour consisted of a glass pot of hot water simmering on a burner and packets of instant coffee. They went through the mechanical routines of emptying the packets into cups, adding hot water, stirring and asking each other polite questions about sugar and cream. The room was empty except for the two of them. There didn't seem to be anything important to say and small talk was somehow pointless.

"Do you think there's any chance she'll make it?" Robyn asked finally.

"You were with her so you're in a better position to answer that question than I am," Trev pointed out. "What do you think?"

Robyn's throat suddenly choked up and all she managed was a negative shake of her head.

They finished their coffee and found a comfortable little waiting room down the hall. Trev went back to talk to the nurse. Robyn knew it was probably foolish of her to stay here. Trev was right. She couldn't do anything. And yet she knew she couldn't just go home and wait for the final telephone call either.

Trev came back without any news. The

night dragged on. A nurse looked in on them, assuring them they were welcome to wait there as long as they wished. The hospital seemed to have a rather lenient attitude toward visitors, for which Robyn was grateful. She read, drank more coffee, dozed, woke once to find the lights dimmed and her jacket carefully tucked around her to keep her warm.

Trev was standing at the big window that looked out on the hall, hands jammed in his pockets. Robyn felt her anger at him soften slightly. If he didn't really care about his grandmother, he wouldn't be staying here keeping this vigil.

She dozed again, neck kinking uncomfortably, jerking awake each time her head fell too far to one side. Vaguely she was aware of something placed under her head and she slept again, more soundly this time.

She came awake slowly as fluorescent tubes in the corridor blinked on and spilled light into the little waiting room. She felt cramped and stiff and yet there was something else too, a sort of safe warmth that made her feel loath to move from her secure position. She moved slightly, snuggling into the comfortable curve of warmth. Her head drooped again, her eyes closing . . .

Then her eyes flew open as she realized it was no pillow her cheek had touched. It was Trev's shoulder and his arm was around her, his hand resting on her hip. His legs were stretched out, and together they were half-sitting, half-lying on the vinyl couch, bodies pressed together in a tangle of clothing.

Robyn felt a sudden rush of shock. How long had they been like this, her body curved intimately against his? Then she was indignant and angry. How dare he!

She struggled to free herself and sit up properly, but in some reflex action of sleep his arm only tightened around her, irresistibly pulling her back against the lean, hard length of his body. It was an unconscious movement, meaningless, and yet suddenly Robyn's breath caught and her heart hammered. She looked up at him, caught by conflicting emotions.

His head was thrown back against the couch, his strong throat exposed. A dark strand of hair lay across his tanned forehead. A day-old beard left a hint of bluish shadow across his angular jaw, a shadow that only emphasized his harsh virility. The hint of beard also emphasized the white line of the scar, and without thinking what she was doing she reached up to run a finger lightly across it.

The touch sent an unexpected shiver through her. Carefully she reached out and tucked the jackets he had evidently placed over them for warmth more closely around the two of them. His body felt warm, hard, reassuring to her touch.

Then, moving cautiously so as not to disturb him, she settled her body back into the hollow of his arm, her head against his chest.

Now why had she done that? she asked herself in annoyance as she listened to the steady, powerful beat of his heart. Why hadn't she jumped up and told him he had a lot of nerve taking advantage of her when she was asleep?

Well, because he was obviously tired too. He needed some rest, she rationalized. And yet she knew that wasn't the real reason, knew there was something else, something new and disturbing she didn't want to face, some desire in her body that had nothing to do with the rational thoughts in her head.

The rhythmic rise and fall of his chest had a hypnotic effect on her. The motion blended with the powerful heartbeat, with the touch of warm breath on her cheek, the drugging warmth of his body next to hers. . . .

She didn't intend to sleep again but she did, coming awake as she felt a stir of movement beside her and then a touch on her hair. She looked up into his blue eyes, her own widening in shock as she realized what she had done.

"I must have dozed off," she said helplessly.

"Have a good night's sleep?" he asked almost lazily.

"Yes — no —," Robyn stammered, flustered by the intimacy of their positions and his evident amusement at her embarrassment. He did not seem in the least disturbed that her arm was draped across his lean waist and her body molded against his as if they were one. Perhaps he was accustomed to waking up in the arms of some near-stranger, she thought angrily, but she certainly was not. "Have you been to check on your grandmother recently?" she asked, trying to keep her voice cool and aloof while she untangled bodies and clothing.

It was a ridiculous question, she realized immediately, since she had the impression they had been sleeping together for hours. Then she felt her face flush. That wasn't what she meant, even in the privacy of her own thoughts. What she meant was . . . oh, forget it, she told herself furiously.

"You might have asked before you — you —" Her voice strangled over the words.

He gave her an amused look as he

stretched his lean frame, making no particular effort to help her in the untangling process. "And you'd have given me an outraged look and a frigid, 'No, thank you,' and we'd have wound up sleeping uncomfortably at opposite ends of the room. Wasn't this a lot more enjoyable?"

Enjoyable! Robyn gasped and felt her face flame. She finally got the sleeve of her jacket untangled from his belt and rose unsteadily to her feet. He gave her an appraising glance and she hurriedly tried to straighten her blouse. Her hair tumbled in her eyes and she tried without success to tidy it with her hands.

Finally Trev stood up, ran a hand through his hair and shook the wrinkles out of his jacket. He didn't look as if he had just spent the night on a sofa in a hospital waiting room. He looked fit and ready.

"Why don't you freshen up in the ladies' room? I'll check on my grandmother and meet you in the cafeteria."

She nodded and fled, glad to be out of his disturbing presence and the even more disturbing memory of their bodies pressed so intimately together. The tempo of hospital routine had increased, and Robyn saw a big metal cart loaded with breakfast trays in the hallway. A nurse carrying a tray of medications moved from room to room with professional efficiency.

Robyn washed her face in the ladies' room, scrubbing with the abrasive pink powder in the metal dispenser until her skin glowed as if she could scrub away the touch of Trev's chest against her cheek. A few strokes of a comb tamed her disheveled hair, but she couldn't find so much as a lipstick in the way of makeup in her purse. Well, she thought grimly, perhaps Trev would be shocked if he saw what his glamorous starlets looked like without all their makeup too.

His eyes flicked over her but he made no comment when he returned. He just said briefly, "There's a doctor with her now. The nurse said we could talk to him in a few minutes. We may as well get something to eat."

Robyn nodded. At least Mrs. Barrone was still alive. She didn't think she would be able to eat at all, but after seeing the scrambled eggs and ham, smelling the aroma of perked coffee, the healthy appetite of youth took over. They ate with little more conversation than they'd had the night before. Which was hardly surprising, Robyn reminded herself. They had little more in common than their rather tenuous relationship through Mrs. Barrone. And, she remembered with a flush of embarrassment, a night spent in each other's arms. Probably not many of Trevor Barrone's all-night partners could boast — or complain? — of such an uneventful night, however, she thought wryly.

Trev ate rapidly and efficiently, Robyn more slowly.

Afterward they went back to the waiting room where the nurse had told Trev the doctor would see them. He was older and grayer than Dr. Helgeson, but what he had to say, after introducing himself as Dr. Martin, was about the same.

"I wish I could be more encouraging," he said regretfully. "But — to be frank, I'm surprised she survived the night."

"Is she conscious?" Trev asked.

"She opened her eyes while I was examining her but I'm not sure she understands what is happening around her."

"May we see her?" Robyn asked.

The doctor hesitated, then nodded. "I can't see that it could do any harm. I'll tell the nurse to let you in for a few minutes."

It was all too obvious from the way he spoke that he was giving them a last chance to see her before she died. Robyn swallowed convulsively, eyes blurring with tears for the woman who had been like a grandmother to her.

Robyn started to follow the doctor out the

door, but Trev held her back until the white-coated figure was gone. She looked at him in surprise. "Don't you want to see her?" she asked.

"Yes, of course I do." He hesitated, dark brows knit in a scowl, and Robyn was reminded of the way he had taken so long to work around to asking the favor of her the day he had come to her shop.

"Would you prefer to see her alone? Is that it?"

"No. I — I had a lot of time to think last night. You're right, of course," he said gruffly. "I should have done more for her while she was alive and healthy and could have enjoyed it."

"Well, it's too late now," Robyn snapped. The words came out sharper than she intended, but she didn't apologize. It was time he realized he hadn't done right by that sweet old woman who adored him.

"Maybe not. Maybe it isn't too late," Trev said slowly. "Not to give her the one thing she wanted most."

Robyn felt puzzled. What could he possibly offer Mrs. Barrone in her present condition? She raised her eyebrows questioningly.

"The thing that always seemed most important to her was seeing I was safely settled down —"

"Securely married to some 'nice, sensible young lady,'" Robyn agreed. "But I don't see how you're going to accomplish that in the next five minutes. Unless on your recent 'business' trip you acquired a wife you haven't bothered to mention."

"Of course not," he growled. "Don't be a fool."

"Then I don't see how —"

"I can't tell her I have a wife," he admitted. He hesitated. "But we could tell her the two of us plan to be married."

Robyn stared at him in openmouthed astonishment before she finally managed to gasp, "You can't be serious! We can't just go in there and *lie* to her."

"Not even to make her last hours happy?" he asked. "Look, what I'm saying is you were right. It is too late to do anything in the way of making life better or easier for her. For once I'm trying to give her more than a — a microwave oven. I'm trying to give her the peace of mind that will come from knowing I'm married, or going to be, to the kind of girl she'd approve of. It's the only thing I can give her now."

"But lying to her — deceiving her —"

"Do you think bringing her happiness in the last few hours of her life isn't worth a small deception?"

"But she may not even be conscious," Robyn protested. "She probably won't understand what you're saying."

A trace of a grim smile touched his mouth. "Then it can't do any harm to go in and say it."

Robyn turned and paced the length of the waiting room. In spite of her doubts about doing what Trev wanted, it did show he had been giving some serious thought to what was really important to his grandmother. It made her see him in a somewhat different light.

"Look, I'm not asking you to do this for me. Do it for *her*. If she's too far gone to understand what we're saying, then that's just the way it is. We're too late. But if she can still understand, she'll —"

"Die happy," Robyn filled in.

"If death can ever be considered happy," Trev conceded wryly.

Robyn paced in the other direction, hands twisting nervously. Deception went against everything in her nature. She didn't like walking in and telling the elderly woman whom she loved a bold-faced lie. And yet, if it really would bring happiness and peace of mind in her dying hours . . .

"What makes you think your grandmother would believe such a story even if she understands what you're saying?" Robyn asked slowly. She paused by the vinyl couch they had shared during the night and lifted her eyes to his.

Trev shrugged, obviously growing impatient. "She thinks you're the greatest girl on earth. Why wouldn't I fall in love with you?"

"Your grandmother is not stupid!" Robyn flared. "She's seen and read enough about you and your starlets to know what sort of woman you prefer. She knows you're hardly the type to consider marrying someone like me!"

But even as she said it, Robyn knew that wasn't completely true. In spite of the book and the gossip columns, Mrs. Barrone still thought of her grandson as the little boy who came to visit, the little boy who buried treasure on the beach and always kept his promises. The kind of man who, when he finally married, just might choose a "nice, sensible girl."

"Why me?" Robyn said slowly. "Why not call in one of the girls you really might marry some day? At least then it wouldn't be a complete lie."

Trev sighed, exasperated with her reluctance. "Obviously there isn't time," he pointed out. Dryly he added, "And, as you seem aware, some of the girls I've been seen with are not exactly the type my grand-mother would consider suitable wife mate-rial."

Robyn was suddenly reminded of that time not so very long ago when Mrs. Barrone had actually said she hoped her grandson would marry a girl just like Robyn. Robyn had considered the idea as hopeless wishful thinking at the time. It seemed even more unlikely now that she knew the man personally. And yet, if Mrs. Barrone really believed it was possible . . .

"As you've pointed out, what my grand-mother approves of is a nice, sensible girl," Trev went on. Cynically he added, "And I'm also sure you could win hands down any 'Nicest Girl in Town' award. You're the kind of girl every mother hopes her son will bring home as his wife."

Robyn stared at him, color rising to her cheeks. "You make being nice sound like some sort of loathsome disease!" she snapped.

He shrugged, and his eyes suddenly nar-rowed in speculation. "Perhaps I was wrong. I thought you would want to do something to make her last hours happy. But maybe you're not so nice after all. How much money will it take to — ah — ease your con-science about a small deceit?"

Robyn just stared at him again, shock and fury strangling her effort to speak. Finally she managed to gasp, "How dare you offer me *money!* I wouldn't take your money if — if —" Words failed her in her fury and she sputtered helplessly.

Trev lifted a dark eyebrow. "Is that a new twist on the old cliché about 'I wouldn't marry you if you were the last man on earth'?"

"You — you're despicable!" All her earlier, kind thoughts about Trev vanished in an explosion of anger. She didn't know why he wanted to play out this farce, but it certainly wasn't because there was anything "nice" about *him.*

"We're not here to discuss my character," he said abruptly, harshly. "Will you do it or won't you?"

"Yes. Yes, I'll do it," Robyn managed to say. "And then I never want to see you again!"

Chapter Four

Had Mrs. Barrone understood?

Robyn's palms felt damp with nervous perspiration as they stepped into the hallway from the intensive care unit, and she suddenly realized she was clutching Trev's hand as if her life depended on it. She released her grip abruptly, though Trev hardly seemed to notice. His face had a set, closed expression, and he turned away before Robyn could see his eyes, as if perhaps he didn't want her to see any emotion exposed there.

Robyn's harsh anger toward him melted slightly. He hadn't been unaffected by their brief meeting with his grandmother. He had been tender with her, his voice gentle and soothing as he told her he and Robyn had fallen in love and would be married very soon. Then he had nodded to Robyn to speak and she had tried until her voice broke with emotion and she couldn't go on.

"Do you think she understood what we were saying?" Trev asked now, cutting into her thoughts.

Robyn hesitated. At first she hadn't thought so. Mrs. Barrone's eyes hadn't opened and her colorless face hadn't moved. She hardly seemed to be breathing. Her frail body was dwarfed by the bed and the jungle of tubes and bottles and trays around her. But when Robyn's voice broke, Mrs. Barrone's veined hand had moved ever so slightly as if she were trying to reach out to them. Both Robyn and Trev had reached for that frail hand and their hands had tangled and then joined with hers in a gesture of unity. Had she smiled then? Yes, Robyn thought, fighting back the tears, she had smiled. Just a bare twitch of the colorless lips perhaps, but a smile, followed by a look of peace, a relaxing of the lines on the wrinkled face.

Robyn nodded. "Yes, I think she understood." And that made it all worthwhile, Robyn thought almost fiercely. So what if it was a deception? An outright lie, if you wanted to be blunt. It had brought Mrs. Barrone happiness and peace of mind and that was all that really mattered right now. And if perhaps she hadn't understood the actual words, at least she knew people who loved her were there.

"Good," Trev said, his voice brisk. If he had felt any emotion, it was gone now. "Mission accomplished then. I'll take you home."

Robyn looked up at him blankly, her eyes still misted with tears. She thought momentarily about arguing with him, telling him she would find her own way home or that she wasn't going home at all, but the effort to resist his will was more than she could muster. She nodded.

His Ferrari was in the parking lot, sleek and gleaming like a beautiful cat. He opened the door and she slid into the bucket seat. In spite of her weariness she was conscious of the luxurious interior. He started the car and pulled smoothly out of the parking lot.

They drove in silence through the corridor of redwoods that flanked the winding highway between Redwood Valley and Caverna Bay, fog drifting in the tops of the towering trees. Robyn's thoughts kept going back over the scene in the hospital. How much longer could Mrs. Barrone last? Not long, that was all too obvious. All they could hope for now was that the end would be painless. And what they had done would make the end more peaceful for her.

"I'm glad we did it," Robyn said in a muffled voice as Trev braked at Caverna Bay's one stoplight. "I really do think she understood and that it made her happy."

Trev didn't comment. "Do you want me

to call you when — if anything happens?"

Robyn realized he was asking the question because of her angry outburst just before they had gone in to see his grandmother. She hesitated. His suggestion about paying her was unforgivable of course, but she had to remember he was under a great deal of stress and strain too. And her earlier attacks on him hadn't been exactly kind. There wasn't any point in continuing that sort of hostile antagonism, she decided. They would still have to see each other at the funeral. They might as well be civil to each other at least. She could invite him in for coffee.

"Well, you seem to have company," Trev observed as he pulled to a stop behind the car already parked in her driveway.

"It's just Larry. Larry McAllister. He's the artist who paints the redwood and ocean scenes I sell in the gift shop. He's probably here to pick up some driftwood mobiles I was supposed to have ready for him." Robyn's voice was hurried and then she was angry with herself for explaining. What did she care what Trev thought?

She slid out of the car just as Larry came around the corner of the building. His glance jumped from Robyn to the sleek car and back again.

"I was beginning to get worried," he said. "I

96

tried to call you late last night, and then when you still weren't home this morning —"

"Something's happened," Robyn cut in hurriedly. "I'll tell you about it later. I'll introduce —" She broke off sharply as the Ferrari suddenly shot out of the driveway.

"Let me guess," Larry said dryly. "That was Trevor Barrone." He glanced at his watch. "Kind of early in the day for a date, isn't it? Or maybe you're just getting in from last night's date?" he added pointedly.

Robyn was still staring after the car. Trev hadn't given her a chance to say, yes, she would like him to call when there was any news about Mrs. Barrone. For a moment she felt a sharp pang of disappointment, and then she resolutely put it down. If that was the way Trevor Barrone wanted to be, it was fine with her. She could call the hospital herself.

"What's going on?" Larry asked, his gaze following Robyn's. "Lovers' quarrel so early in the game?"

For a moment Robyn felt an unreasoning stab of anger at Larry. If he hadn't been here when they arrived . . .

She fought the feeling down and briefly, without emotion, told him what had happened, leaving out only the part about what she and Trev had told Mrs. Barrone. That, she decided grimly, was something she would never tell anyone. For Mrs. Barrone's sake she wasn't sorry she had done it, but there was no need for anyone else to know about the deception.

Larry looked chagrined when she was through. "I feel like a damn fool," he muttered. "You've been through all this and here I am making noises like a jealous boyfriend. And you've already made it plain I'm 'just a friend' so I don't have the right to be jealous even if you'd spent the night sleeping with him," he admitted.

And that, Robyn thought guiltily, was another little point she'd glossed over. She hadn't exactly mentioned just *how* she had spent the night in that hospital waiting room with Trev. Not that it meant anything anyway, she assured herself firmly. She hadn't even realized she was sleeping in his arms until she woke up. And it surely didn't mean anything to Trev.

She strode toward the door, resolutely putting all that out of her mind. "The mobiles are all finished," she said over her shoulder to Larry. "It will take only a few minutes to get them packed and ready."

"No hurry."

They went inside. Larry, comfortably familiar with her small quarters, turned up the heat and made coffee while Robyn showered and changed. She didn't know if her clothes looked slept in, but they certainly felt that way. She slipped into comfortable, chocolate colored velour pants and shirt, applied some light makeup and felt considerably refreshed by the time she went out to accept the hot coffee Larry offered.

"I'll get busy on those mobiles —"

"Relax," he said. "You look beat. Beautiful," he amended, "but still beat." He paused. "Mrs. Barrone isn't going to make it, I gather?"

Robyn took a sip of coffee, then shook her head. "It's my fault," she said unhappily. "If I'd gone over when I should have, she wouldn't have tried to move those plants around herself."

"But you said the doctor thought she'd had a stroke," Larry pointed out. "It could have happened whether she was moving the plants or not."

"But if I'd found her sooner —"

"Look, stop blaming yourself," Larry said almost roughly. "Where was the great author all this time? Why wasn't he there to move her damn plants or find her after she fell?"

Yes, *where was he?* Robyn repeated slowly to herself as she sipped the hot coffee. She

99

moved her feet closer to the warmth of the gas stove.

"He said he was out of town on business," she said, repeating the curt statement Trev had made earlier.

Larry laughed shortly. "What do you want to bet Trevor Barrone's 'business' had a name like Lola or Debbie or —"

"He hasn't any reason to lie or sneak around," Robyn snapped. "No one is keeping tabs on him." Privately she suspected exactly what Larry was saying, but somehow she found it grating to hear him say it in so many words.

Larry's eyebrows lifted. "Oh ho, what is this? Did I hit a sore spot?"

Robyn set the cup down. "Look, I just find this all rather tasteless right now," she said firmly. "Mrs. Barrone is dying and that is all I'm concerned about."

Larry was immediately apologetic again. Guiltily Robyn realized she had used Mrs. Barrone's condition to avoid any further discussion about Trev, discussion that she found oddly disturbing, though she couldn't explain why even to herself. It was certainly no concern of hers what kind of "business" Trevor Barrone conducted, except that this particular trip had had such disastrous consequences for Mrs. Barrone.

Briskly she set about packaging the mobiles in individual boxes, labeling them with her own "Robyn Christopher Creation" labels with the distinctive little red-breasted robin emblem. When the mobiles were boxed, Larry carried them out to his car.

At her door he said awkwardly, "I'm sorry. I know I don't have any right to ask nosy questions." He gave her a slightly crooked grin. "I suppose it's just that I'm still hoping that someday —"

Robyn stretched up to give him an impulsive kiss on the cheek. "You're my very best friend, and I don't even *like* Trevor Barrone."

"Sometimes you don't have to really like someone to fall in love," Larry said slowly.

"Now that is a — a *dumb* statement if I ever heard one," Robyn said spiritedly. "Trev and I —"

"See? Now you're calling him *Trev*," Larry pointed out. "That sounds pretty familiar to me."

Robyn shook her head and laughed. "You're impossible." She started to close the door, but he blocked it with his foot.

"Just don't forget my warning about Trevor Barrone," he said.

Robyn laughed and waved him off. What she had said to Larry was true. She *didn't* like Trev. Oh sure, he was good-looking and

101

had a certain virility that was attractive — *very* attractive — in a blatantly physical way. But she hadn't liked him before she met him and she didn't like him now. Especially not after he'd made that crude suggestion about paying her, and even more especially after his abrupt departure today. That was rude to both her and Larry, and totally uncalled-for, she thought, suddenly angry with him again.

She wandered through the small rooms restlessly. She didn't feel like sitting down in her workshop and tackling the painstaking work that making the agate and shell jewelry required. It would be a good day for going to the beach but she didn't want to be away from the phone. She went around front and picked up her mail. There were some business letters that should be answered but she didn't feel like doing that either.

She suddenly wondered if Trev had gone back to the hospital or if he was over at Mrs. Barrone's house. She could just wander over that way, say she thought she'd come over and straighten up the mess in the living room. Then she stopped short, aghast. What was she thinking? She didn't want to see Trev again. Her outburst at the hospital might have been childish, but it was certainly accurate. She did *not* want to see him again.

The phone shrilled and Robyn raced for it. "Hello?" she said breathlessly.

It was only Mrs. Barrone's friend Mabel wanting to know how she was. Word had gotten around quickly that Mrs. Barrone had been taken to the hospital. Mabel was blaming herself too, saying she should have checked on Rose. Robyn soothed her, assuring her she mustn't feel guilty.

Robyn poured another cup of coffee after the phone call. Then she stretched out on the floor beside the gas heater, one of her handmade throw pillows under her head, and the phone within arm's reach. Through the window looking out on the park she could see the old redwood stump with the walkway cut through it. It was a favorite haunt of the neighborhood children. Had Trev played there when he was a little boy? she wondered idly.

There, she was doing it again, she thought, catching herself angrily. Thinking about Trev. Why? Why was he always there in her mind? Even now, as she was angry with him for his rude departure, another part of her was remembering the feel of his lean, hard body molded against hers, remembering the powerful heartbeat against her ear, remembering the quickening thud of her own heartbeat. How could she feel even a momentary physical attraction for such an arrogant, cold, materialistic man?

And yet he hadn't been cold or harsh when he was telling his grandmother about their forthcoming "marriage." What if that hadn't been just a pretense? Robyn wondered dreamily. What if it were for real? What if Trev really were in love with her? What if they really were planning to be married . . . live together . . . raise a family . . .

A slow, unfamiliar flood of warmth spread through her as visions drifted through her mind. Trev's kiss . . . Trev's touch, trailing fire across her body . . . Trev making love to her, eyes dark with passion.

Robyn sat up abruptly, shocked and horrified at the turn her thoughts had taken. Here she was, daydreaming like some infatuated adolescent! And all over a man she would probably never see again, except across a room at a funeral, a man for whom she felt only scorn and anger.

Briskly she bounced to her feet and in a flurry of activity she answered the mail, whisked through a quick housecleaning and caught up on the gift shop bookkeeping. The activity more or less managed to keep her mind off both Trev and Mrs. Barrone. Later she fixed a light soup-and-salad supper, her glance darting frequently to the owl-shaped clock on the wall. Trev would call, wouldn't he, when something happened? He wouldn't cold-bloodedly leave her to wonder?

Yes, she decided unhappily, when there was still no word by almost nine o'clock. He just might be that cold-blooded. She dialed the hospital and got a rather vague report that there was "No change" in Mrs. Barrone's condition. So there really hadn't been any reason for Trev to call, she thought slowly as she hung up. But he should have called anyway, she decided, anger returning in that odd seesaw of emotions he seemed to arouse in her. "No change" was really news, considering that they had hardly expected her to live through the day.

She felt a surge of hope. Was it really possible the doctors might bring Mrs. Barrone through? There were so many things doctors could do today, new medicines, new equipment, new techniques. On sudden impulse she dialed Mrs. Barrone's home number, thinking Trev might be there. Surely he could tell her more than the hospital's rather noncommittal statement.

She let the phone ring a long time, but there was no answer and finally she hung up, spirits drooping again. Mrs. Barrone's condition had been nearly hopeless this morning. The doctor had said as much. "No change" didn't mean she was going to pull through. It just meant the end hadn't come yet.

Robyn stayed up, head nodding over a book, until almost eleven o'clock, hoping Trev would call with something more specific to report, but finally she gave up and went to bed. Sleep came quickly but it was filled with dreams, half-wakings, nightmares. Visions of Mrs. Barrone, the peaceful look on her face suddenly shattered into horror as an unseen voice shouted, "Lies! Lies! It's all lies!" Dreams of Trev, sometimes harsh and cold, sometimes warm and tender. The pillow beneath her head turned into his shoulder and when she looked up his mouth dipped to meet hers, and she felt the passion in his body. . . .

She woke groggily, aware of a buzzing in her head that finally translated into the ringing of the telephone. She reached for the bedside phone, struggling to separate reality from dreams.

"Hello?"

"Did I wake you?" With characteristic arrogance Trev didn't bother to identify himself or apologize for the early call. Robyn tried to focus her eyes on the bedside clock. Eight o'clock. It wasn't all that early. She should have been up an hour ago.

"I was just getting up," she white-lied. "I tried to call you at your grandmother's house last night but there was no answer."

"I've taken a room at a motel near the hospital. They just let me in to see her for a few minutes."

"She's still alive?" Robyn gasped. She straightened up in bed, propping the pillow behind her. She ran a hand through her disheveled hair. "How is she?"

"Holding her own, surprisingly. I think she'd like to see you."

"You think?"

"She's too weak to say more than a word or two. The stroke has affected her speech slightly."

"Then this doesn't mean —"

"That she is going to recover? No," he said flatly. "It just means we have to keep up our charade a little longer."

Robyn's heart flip-flopped. "You think she remembers what we told her?"

"I don't know. It's hard to say." He paused. "Don't you want her to remember?"

"Yes, of course I do. As you pointed out, a certain peace of mind about your future is about all we can do for her now."

"Did you tell your friend Larry about this?" Trev remarked unexpectedly.

"Of course not," Robyn said indignantly. "This is just among the — the three of us." What did he think, that she would go around bragging she was "engaged" to a famous author? She had a sudden, angry suspicion that in spite of his concern for his grandmother he might be a little amused by this situation. He probably thought he was giving her a real thrill. "I'll be over as soon as I can get ready," she finished crisply.

"Good. I'll see you later then."

Robyn slumped back in the bed for a minute after hanging up the phone, feeling a little disoriented by the jarring transition from sleeping to waking. And she blushed to remember what she had been dreaming when the phone wakened her. Mrs. Barrone might not think she was such a "nice, sensible girl" if she knew about that dream!

She dressed in a neat blouse with standup collar and belted pants and hurried through a cornflakes breakfast. It was less than forty-five minutes after Trev's call when she guided her economy compact car out of the carport. The sky was clear today, the wind brisk. She fought the urge to drive the winding, redwood-lined road to Redwood Valley faster than her usual speed. Her tires were getting a little thin and this, of all days, was no time to have a blowout or accident.

Trev's Ferrari was in the hospital parking lot when she pulled in. She went to the main hospital entrance this time. Trev met her, as if he had been waiting and watching for her. Their eyes met, held, and Robyn's glance dropped first. He hadn't wanted to call her this morning, she suspected, perhaps wouldn't have if his grandmother hadn't asked for her.

"May we see her now?" Robyn asked coolly.

"Not now. At least there isn't any point in seeing her now. She's sleeping. Or maybe it's a coma. I don't know. I'm not sure they do." He sounded uncharacteristically agitated. "If I could just get her down to the Daydecker Clinic in San Francisco —" He broke off, ran a hand through his hair, then got control of himself again. "I should have waited to call you," he said stiffly. "No need for you to rush over so early."

"I don't mind," Robyn said. She gave him a sideways glance. "You rushed off in somewhat of a hurry yourself yesterday morning."

"You had company." He looked down at her, blue eyes appraising. "I drove by again later, but your friend's car was still there."

Robyn was surprised to hear he had come back. "I'm sorry —" she began.

He cut her off curtly. "It doesn't matter."

They went to the same small lounge

where they had spent the night and waited again. They drank coffee, flipped through well-worn magazines and carried on an occasional scrap of desultory conversation. Trev said he had arranged to have the window repaired and the living room cleaned up in Mrs. Barrone's house. Robyn sat in an uncomfortable straight-backed chair and tried to keep her eyes and mind away from the couch they had shared that night. She still couldn't reconcile her scorn and distaste for Trevor Barrone with the odd shiver of excitement that ran through her whenever she thought about that night.

Had he given that night any thought? she wondered. No, she decided wryly. His idea of spending a night with a woman surely included more fireworks than that. And yet no one had forced him to hold her in his arms, and he hadn't seemed in any big hurry to extricate himself the next morning.

They lunched at the cafeteria. Robyn felt drowsy afterward but she held her body rigidly erect in the straight chair. No more of that foolishness.

About midafternoon a nurse stuck her head in and said they could see Mrs. Barrone for just a minute. Outside the intensive care unit Trev stopped and deliberately took Robyn's hand in his.

"We're supposed to be engaged, you know. We have to make it look good." His voice was mocking but with an undertone that was almost threatening.

Robyn hesitated. Maybe what they were doing wasn't right. Maybe deceiving someone in the last hours of her life was all wrong. Maybe that was the time for total honesty.

"What's wrong?" Trev asked sharply as Robyn hesitated.

"I don't know. I just —" She broke off as a strange thought occurred to her. What if Mrs. Barrone didn't die? How would they explain all this then? Trev was looking down at her, eyes narrowed. "I — I'm just not very good at this sort of thing," she faltered.

"I don't think anyone ever gets 'very good' at confronting death," he said. His voice was unemotional but not unkind. His grip on her hand felt damp and she had the sudden feeling that he wasn't as calm about all this as he pretended to be.

Robyn steeled herself for the first sight of Mrs. Barrone, but it came as a shock anyway. The thin, almost transparent skin with the veins so vulnerably prominent on her temples, the gash cleaned but unbandaged. The frail body barely wrinkling the smooth covers, the needle taped to the thin arm. Could she really have shrunk so much in the last few days? Robyn wondered, blinking back tears. Or was it just that her feisty personality always made you forget how tiny and fragile she really was? She was still surrounded by the jungle of tubes and bottles, and now there was a big, shiny steel machine behind her too, ominous with dials and switches.

Robyn and Trev stood there motionless, hands clasped. Finally Robyn whispered, "I think she's —"

The eyelids fluttered open and Robyn caught her breath as Mrs. Barrone's faded blue eyes, unfocused at first, finally settled first on Trev and then moved slowly to Robyn. Trev reached out and took her hand in both of his.

"Grandma, it's Trev. Trev and Robyn."

Grandma. Robyn had never heard him use the term before. He had always used the colder, more formal "my grandmother" when speaking of her to Robyn, and she found the endearing term oddly touching.

"Do you remember what I told you? Robyn and I are going to be married." He reached back and pulled Robyn up beside him, slipping his arm around her as if afraid she might decide to turn and run.

"That's right," Robyn said shakily. She clasped Mrs. Barrone's withered hand too.

"We're going to be married. And we're going to have a big wedding, and you're going to get well and come to it. There will be baskets and baskets of flowers and you'll wear an orchid corsage."

Now why was she saying all that? Robyn wondered wildly. It was all so impossible. And yet the words just seemed to come, tumbling over each other as she built the impossible dream. Mrs. Barrone's eyes drifted closed but there was the trace of a smile on her face as if she, too, were seeing the baskets of flowers, the bride in white, the orchid corsage.

Finally Robyn's voice trailed off and Mrs. Barrone opened her eyes again. Her lips moved, straining to speak.

Trev touched her withered cheek. "Don't, Grandma. There's no need to say anything."

Her lips moved again, determination forcing a whisper through them. "I'm — so happy — two people I love most — love each other."

The words were slurred, as if one side of her mouth were stiff, but the trace of a smile was there again.

"We're happy too, Grandma," Trev said. His voice was husky with emotion. His arm tightened around Robyn though she doubted he was even aware of it.

"— sudden —" Mrs. Barrone murmured.

Trev glanced at Robyn. "What did she say?" he whispered.

"I think she thinks this is all kind of sudden," Robyn said. Leave it to Mrs. Barrone, Robyn thought ruefully. She always had been sharp as a tack. Even in her present condition the suddenness of this great "love" hadn't escaped her.

"It may look as if it's sudden, but it really isn't," Trev said. "I've been looking all my life for a girl like Robyn. No, not *like* her. I've been looking for Robyn herself. I just didn't know her name until I got here and found you had her safely hidden away for me where no one else could find her. And now that I've found her I'm never going to let her get away."

Robyn felt her breath catch as he spoke. The words could have come out saccharine sweet, sticky and unbelievable, but he said them harshly, almost fiercely. If she didn't know they were a complete fabrication, she might even have believed he really meant them, and the thought made her feel suddenly shaky. He shot her a dark glance, as if defying her to disagree with him.

Mrs. Barrone just lay there and Robyn thought she had drifted beyond their reach again. Then her fingers made a little scrabbling motion on the bedsheets. Trev touched

114

her hand reassuringly but still the fingers moved.

"— show me —"

"What is it?" Trev turned to Robyn, his face alarmed. "What's wrong? Should I call the nurse?"

Robyn reached out and touched the thin hand again. She leaned closer as Mrs. Barrone struggled to squeeze another word out.

"— ring —"

And then Robyn realized what Mrs. Barrone wanted. To her old-fashioned mind a pledge to wed meant an engagement ring. Even now Mrs. Barrone still wore the tiny diamond in its antique filigree setting that her beloved husband had given her many years ago. Robyn looked at Trev helplessly.

"She wants to see my engagement ring."

Trev looked at her a moment, mouth set, then turned back to his grandmother. "We haven't had time to pick one out yet," he said smoothly. "We've been pretty concerned about you, you know."

"I'm — old bother."

Robyn leaned over and smoothed the white hair. The faded eyes followed her face weakly. "You're no bother at all. You just hurry and get well for our — our wedding."

"— plants —"

"Your plants are just fine," Trev said quickly. "I have someone coming in to water them. And move them around too."

Robyn glanced at him, surprised and touched by his thoughtfulness. In all this, she hadn't given a single thought to the plants, and yet, of course, Mrs. Barrone would worry about them.

After the effort of getting the few words out, Mrs. Barrone's face relaxed peacefully, eyes closed. The faint smile hovered on her lips. Everything was taken care of, that smile seemed to say. Her plants watered and moved, her grandson settled down. She looked beautiful, Robyn thought with a painful tug at her heart. Thin, fragile as fine porcelain, but beautiful. Robyn held her breath. Was she gone, drifting peacefully away?

No. The frail chest moved in a shallow breath. Robyn held her own breath again as it seemed so long before another breath came. Her hand felt damp with nervous perspiration.

"I think we'd better leave her alone now," Trev whispered. His voice sounded as strained as Robyn felt.

She didn't resist the firm hand on her elbow as he guided her out to the hallway. She blinked, a little dazed, as if she had just come back from some other world. A nurse, hovering just behind them, pulled the green curtain around the bed. In the hallway a man went by pushing a cart loaded with dirty trays and dishes. A light pulsed softly over a doorway. Two doctors went by discussing the medical convention in San Francisco.

All these people just going about their jobs, Robyn thought wonderingly, and others were dying. . . . She lifted her eyes to Trev's. She thought his were suspiciously moist, but he looked away before she could be sure. "That was very thoughtful of you to arrange for someone to care for her plants. I know it made her feel better."

His jaw tightened. He propelled her to one side to let an aide pushing a cart of fresh linens pass by. "I'll get someone," he said briefly.

"So that was all just a lie too!" she said with bitter disillusionment. "Isn't anything about you real?"

He lifted a dark eyebrow. "Were all the things you said real?" he retorted.

"No, of course not, but —" She floundered helplessly.

"They almost sounded real. If I didn't know better, I'd think you were madly in love with me." He laughed humorlessly. "In

117

fact, you really gave a great performance. All that flowery description of the wedding, right down to the orchid corsage. Sounded as if you'd been planning it for years. I'm sure you could win the award of the year for 'Best Performance in a Hospital.' "

Robyn stared at him angrily. And she had thought perhaps he really felt something when he was in there with his grandmother. "I'll put it with my 'Nicest Girl in Town' award," she said sarcastically.

"You mustn't be greedy," he chided.

She gave him one more scathing look and then started down the hallway. He caught up with her in one long stride and his steel grip yanked her to a halt.

"Let go of me. I'm going home." She tried to pull away but his hand only tightened painfully around her arm.

"Not yet. There's a little job we have to do first."

"Now what?" she said bitterly. "Find some innocent kids and tell them a few lies just for the fun of it?"

He ignored her outburst. "Now," he said grimly, "we get a ring."

Chapter Five

Robyn protested, arguing that there was no point in carrying things that far, but Trev was grimly determined. Finally, shrugging, Robyn gave in.

They went to Redwood Valley's only jewelry store. Robyn didn't make even a pretense of being interested as the salesman brought out trays of glittering rings. She tapped her fingers on the glass display case, impatient for this ridiculous farce to be over. No, no, that wasn't true, she reminded herself hastily, because when it was over that meant Mrs. Barrone would be gone too. No, all she meant was that she was impatient for the farce here in the jewelry store to end.

She had expected Trev would walk in, simply point to a ring and that would be it, but he didn't. He looked critically at the trays of rings and finally the salesman brought out several spectacular rings individually displayed on black velvet. Trev turned to Robyn.

"Have you a preference?" he asked.

She shrugged indifferently.

He selected one and the salesman deferentially asked Robyn to slip it on for sizing. Suddenly Robyn realized it was not one ring, but two, a complete wedding set.

"We won't be needing the wedding band," she said icily.

The salesman was taken aback and murmured something about not being able to break up these sets of specially designed rings.

"Then we don't want —" Robyn began.

"We'll take the set," Trev cut in smoothly. To Robyn's furious glance he remarked mockingly, "I understand diamonds are an excellent investment these days."

Robyn turned away in disgust. He wasn't doing this for his grandmother at all. He was only using money again to soothe his own guilty conscience. Assuming he had a conscience. And now he was cold-bloodedly looking at the rings as an "investment," ever ready to further his own interests even in this unhappy situation.

"Of course you can always use them for your real wedding," she said caustically. "Providing your fiancée doesn't mind one slightly used engagement ring."

The salesman looked bewildered by the biting exchange, but he had evidently learned not to question customers' motives, especially those of customers who were buying one of the most expensive items in the store. He discreetly turned his shoulder to Robyn so he could discuss price with Trev. The salesman at first said it would take several days to have the rings sized to fit Robyn's slim finger, but Trev said flatly that he wanted the rings the following day and that was that. For some people, Robyn thought with an odd mixture of disgust and admiration, things could always be done a little more quickly.

As things turned out, however, the ring did not go on display for Mrs. Barrone the following day. Trev called about noon, just as Robyn was dressing to drive over to the hospital, to say his grandmother had taken a turn for the worse. She had suddenly started having problems breathing and was now in an oxygen tent. There was nothing Robyn could do, he said unemotionally, and no point in her coming over.

Robyn hung up the phone saddened. This was it then. It was only a matter of time now.

The day dragged on. Robyn jumped whenever the phone rang, but it was only Mrs. Barrone's elderly friends checking on her condition. She tried calling Larry at the little apartment-studio where he did his painting, but there was no answer. She wondered how Trev spent his time. Surely he didn't hang around the hospital all day. Perhaps, for Mrs. Barrone's sake, she should have invited him over for dinner. He must be getting tired of hospital cafeteria food.

Robyn decided to hike over to the beach. She couldn't do anything for Mrs. Barrone now, and it would scarcely matter if she got the bad news the moment it happened or an hour or two later.

She loved to walk on the beach. It always gave her a sense of perspective and put her problems into place as she compared them with the timeless crash of the waves, the endless shiftings of the sands, the patient wearing away of solid rock. She could always feel her tensions relaxing, her annoyances evaporating.

But today, in spite of an afternoon that she suddenly realized was glorious with sunshine and exhilarating breezes, she felt neither relaxed nor soothed. She wanted to forget about Trev and yet the first thing she saw on the beach was that gnarled stump from which he had rescued her, flung high and dry on the beach now. In her pocket she even felt the fishline he had broken and tossed to her. A seagull squawked overhead. Possibly the same one he had released, she thought sourly. Why did everything make her think of him?

Determinedly she scrambled over the sharp ridge of rocks separating the crescent of sand from the next stretch of beach. In further exasperation she realized this only brought her to the water-carved cave where Trev had said he had once buried his "treasure" of marbles and pocket knife. She walked on by the cave, not stopping as she usually did to wonder dreamily if some long ago pirate had once stood there also. Concentrating on looking for useful bits of driftwood and shells, she walked on up the beach. But either the sea was being unusually stingy with them, or she was being unusually hard to please, because she returned disconsolately to the house with only a handful of pieces that really didn't please her at all.

By the next morning Trev still hadn't called. She thought about telephoning the hospital for information but after lunch decided to drive over instead.

Trev's Ferrari was in the parking lot. Maybe he really did spend all his time here, Robyn thought wonderingly. To her surprise the reception desk informed her Mrs. Barrone had been moved to a private room. She followed the receptionist's directions through the rambling corridors to number 168.

She hesitated outside, hearing the low

murmur of Trev's voice, then peered around the partly open door. Mrs. Barrone's head was turned toward the door, a rapt expression on her face as if whatever Trev was saying was utterly fascinating. The jungle of bottles and tubes had followed her here, but somehow they looked less ominous in the bright, airy room. Trev was leaning toward his grandmother, his back to Robyn, his strong hands clasping the frail ones.

It was such a close, intimate scene that Robyn was loath to interrupt. She pulled back, but not quickly enough. Mrs. Barrone had seen her. Almost reluctantly she stepped into the room.

Mrs. Barrone smiled. Robyn was astonished to see that it was a real smile, not that ghostly little twitch of the lips that she had earlier rather desperately taken to be a smile. Mrs. Barrone's eyes were not exactly bright, but they no longer had that vague, unfocused look.

"Mrs. Barrone! I didn't know — I'm so pleased! You look marvelous." That wasn't exactly true, but the improvement was remarkable. Robyn's gaze flew to meet Trev's.

"Robyn! How nice to see you, darling. I tried to call you just before I came to the hospital but you must already have been on your way over here." His voice sounded phony, almost forced, and his look was hardly welcoming.

He rose and met Robyn with a kiss on the cheek before she could go to Mrs. Barrone. She looked up at him in astonishment.

"We're engaged, remember?" he muttered grimly. "At least look as if you're glad to see me."

"Why didn't you call me earlier?" she retorted in a whisper.

"I couldn't pick up the ring until just a few minutes ago. The jeweler called in sick." So, the mighty author couldn't control everything after all, she thought as he fumbled in his breast pocket. "Get the damn thing on before she sees you don't have it."

Robyn lifted her hands as if straightening his collar, and he managed to slip the ring on her finger out of Mrs. Barrone's view. Then he turned back to his grandmother, smiling broadly, at ease now.

"Sorry, I just had to have the first kiss. Now she's all yours."

Robyn leaned over and kissed the soft, withered cheek gently. A nurse bustled in and adjusted something on the tube leading to Mrs. Barrone's arm.

"Never give — old woman — any peace," Mrs. Barrone grumbled, eyeing the busy nurse. "Always — fussing."

Her words were slow but less slurred than earlier, Robyn noted, and they seemed to show some of her old, feisty spirit. Trev had said his grandmother was in an oxygen tent and here she was breathing on her own. And not in the intensive care unit either.

"I'm just so surprised," Robyn said. "Trev said you had a — a bit of a relapse."

"Silly doctors thought I —" Mrs. Barrone paused, breath giving out before she finished the sentence. "Thought I was dying."

"You're not dying," Robyn protested. She hoped the statement didn't sound as doubtful as she felt.

"But I just kept telling myself —" Pause. Breath. "I wouldn't die. I kept telling myself — I would *not* die before you two — were married."

"You won't die. You're going to live to see us married. You're going to live a long, long time yet. You'll hold your great-grandchild in your arms —"

Robyn glanced up to see Trev regarding her with a mocking, cynical look on his face, and she was suddenly horrified with herself. Why in the world had she made such a ridiculous statement?

Now Trev stepped up beside her and put his arm around her. His hand moved lightly, caressingly, up and down her arm. "We'll have at least three, won't we, darling?" He smiled at her intimately.

Robyn glared up at him, lips compressed furiously. How could he do this? How could he say these things? It was a mockery, a travesty. She had said what she did without thought, simply chattering on to cheer a sick, elderly woman, but Trev was deliberately playing with both of them. His lips brushed her hair and she fought an urge to slap a stinging palm across his face. And yet even as she fought that urge there was another diametrically opposed feeling, one that was even more disturbing. The slow caress on her arm left a trail of fire that seemed to ignite something deep within her. The intimate smile made her legs feel like melted plastic. The blue eyes burned into hers, suggesting a passion that unexpectedly sent her mind and senses reeling.

She forced herself to look away, to say with counterfeit brightness to Mrs. Barrone, "Have you seen my engagement ring?"

She thrust her hand out so Mrs. Barrone could see. It was the first time Robyn had really looked at the ring too. She had deliberately ignored it in the jewelry store. Now the huge diamond flanked by a swirl of smaller stones made Robyn's breath catch. It really was beautiful. A modern yet graceful design that she really might have chosen for herself. Not that what she thought mattered, of course, she realized grimly. Trev had purchased the rings with an eye to their value as an investment, and large stones were certainly the best investment.

"Lovely," Mrs. Barrone murmured approvingly.

"Nothing but the best for my girl," Trev agreed.

His arm was still around her. Robyn frowned at him, willing him to remove it, but he only smiled and moved his hand down to encircle her waist. He was deliberately toying with her, she thought angrily, amusing himself with her fury and frustration. He knew full well she was powerless to say anything. She could hardly snap, "Get your hands off me," to this man she was supposed to be so madly in love with. And Mrs. Barrone was beaming at them in full approval of Trev's show of affection.

Determinedly Robyn ignored the arm around her waist and the feel of his hard thigh against hers. She chattered on about the people who had called to inquire about Mrs. Barrone's health, talked about going to the beach, even mumbled something about the weather.

Trev moved around behind her, encircling her with his arms and clasping his hands together at her waist, his chin resting intimately against her temple. Robyn knew it was all phony, an elaborate display of affection for Mrs. Barrone's benefit — with perhaps the added plus of furnishing Trev with some sort of private wicked amusement — but it affected her anyway. His warm breath on her ear was distracting, the feel of his powerful chest against her back disturbed her even breathing. She had the feeling she was babbling inanely.

She pulled Trev's locked hands apart and stepped out of his embrace. A little breathlessly she said, "Dear me, here I am running on and you two were having such a nice talk before I arrived."

"Good — to see you," Mrs. Barrone murmured approvingly. "Good to see you — so happy together."

Oh, yes, we're real little lovebirds, Robyn thought grimly. She carefully kept her eyes away from Trev's, knowing the mocking amusement she'd see there. She moved around on the other side of Mrs. Barrone, putting the high hospital bed between herself and Trev. "How are you feeling?" she asked brightly. "I mean, are they treating you right?"

"Doctor said surgery — my hip."

Robyn's glance flew to Trev. Did that mean they thought Mrs. Barrone was well enough to undergo surgery now?

"Yes, they've decided they can't postpone it any longer," Trev said noncommittally.

Robyn studied him uneasily, suspecting this was not particularly good news after all. She was even more certain when Trev abruptly changed the conversation back to a more cheerful subject.

"We'll have to get you a new dress for the wedding. That's what you'd better be thinking about," he said jovially.

Mrs. Barrone plucked at the bedcovers with a frail hand, her eyes suddenly watery. "If only I could be there," she said wistfully. "But I — I'm here — like this."

"You will be there. We couldn't do it without you," Trev said earnestly. He squeezed her veined hand. "Look, you come through this surgery with flying colors and we'll have the wedding right here, right in this hospital room. Minister and everything. Maybe they'll even let you drink a glass of champagne."

Mrs. Barrone's lips parted in wonderment, and Robyn could almost see something come to life within her. For a moment she had looked so dejected and forlorn, but now she was alive again. Her eyes almost had a sparkle. Trev glanced at Robyn, as if again defying her to deny what he had just said.

"That — that's right," Robyn agreed shakily. "Right here in this very room."

Trev leaned over and kissed his grandmother. "Now you just think about that and get some rest. We'll be in to see you again."

Robyn kissed her too. Mrs. Barrone's eyes were closed now, as if the excitement had wearied her, but it was a contented weariness. Trev quietly pulled the door shut behind them as they slipped out.

Robyn turned to face him, her eyes stormy with held back anger. "I agreed to go through with this," she said coldly, "but I will not stand for being pawed!"

He smiled lazily. "Don't you think she'd be a little suspicious if we were something less than — ah — loving?"

"But we can't keep doing this!" Robyn cried wildly. "You have her hoping, *believing* . . ."

"That's the idea," he said. "Hope and belief. It's all we can give her."

"But it's going too far! First the ring and now this, telling her we'll be married in her room."

"If your conscience is bothering you, go back in and tell her it's all a lie," he said harshly. Brutally he added, "Send her into surgery with nothing to live for."

Robyn stared up into those blue eyes, frigid as an Arctic sea now. She couldn't do that, of course, and he knew it. It could be giving Mrs. Barrone a death sentence. Major surgery held its risks at any time of life, but at Mrs. Barrone's age and in her condition the risks were many times multiplied. Spirit and hope were about all that could bring her through.

Realizing he had made his point and won, Trev went on less harshly, explaining the reasons why the doctors had decided they must go ahead with the surgery at this time in spite of the risks. They walked slowly down the hallway and into the slight drizzle falling on the parking lot. Robyn was careful to keep a healthy distance between herself and Trev. The surgery was scheduled for early morning, day after next, Trev said, barring further complications between now and then.

"I'll be here," Robyn said.

"There's no need —"

"I'll be here," Robyn repeated doggedly. They were at her car by now. Robyn reached for the door handle and saw the diamond ring glittering on her left hand. She slipped it off.

"Here. You'd better take care of this. I wouldn't want something to happen to your valuable investment."

"I'd like you to keep it on." Gently, but firmly, he slid the ring back on her finger.

Robyn looked up, surprised, her heart unexpectedly fluttering as his touch sent an involuntary shiver of excitement through her.

"I've arranged with my grandmother's friend, Mabel, to take care of the plants, and Mabel said she might also come to the hospital if visitors were allowed. My grandmother will be sure to say something about our 'plans,' and it might look a little peculiar if Mabel then saw you without the ring. Old ladies tend to notice those things," he added cynically.

"I see," Robyn murmured dryly. "You do think of everything." Then another disturbing thought struck her. "But this means — I mean, other people are going to think —"

"I don't give a damn what other people think." His voice was coldly contemptuous.

"But surely you don't intend to carry out this charade in front of the whole town, in front of everyone!" she gasped.

"I'll do whatever I have to to keep my grandmother alive," he said grimly. "It may not be obvious to you, but I care a great deal about her."

Their eyes met, his darkly challenging, and Robyn knew he had won again. The pretense had spread beyond the hospital room now. The proof was right there on her finger. What would Larry think? She'd have to confide in him, of course. She couldn't let him think this was a real engagement. And yet, reluctantly, she realized that sometimes Larry did tend to be a bit too talkative, especially when he gossiped with the waitresses at Mama-Jo's restaurant. Suppose he made a joke of it and somehow it all got back to Mrs. Barrone? No, she couldn't risk that.

Fortunately, she saw nothing of Larry the following day so there were no uncomfortable explanations to be made. Robyn stayed close to home. For Mrs. Barrone's sake she intended to carry out her part in this charade, but she saw no need to go out and advertise her "engagement." The big diamond felt like a weight on her hand, an unfamiliar object that glittered accusingly at her as she tried to work on the inexpensive little jewelry items she created or went about her everyday chores. She felt that if she went out, everyone would be sure to see the ring and ask questions.

Oh, she would be so glad when this was all over and Trev went away and she could get him out of her mind! And then she remembered in horror that if she was wishing that she was also wishing for Mrs. Barrone's death, because the two were inextricably entwined. No, she didn't want that at all! How could she even have such thoughts?

She drove over to the hospital the following evening but saw Mrs. Barrone, already drowsy from a pill, only for a minute. Trev was not around, though an aide said Robyn had just missed him. The wide-eyed young aide referred to him as Trev, not Mr. Barrone. Spreading his charm around, no doubt, she thought contemptuously.

The next morning Robyn was at the hospital before seven. The receptionist wasn't even on duty yet. A nurse waved Robyn on by. They knew her here now. It was all becoming so familiar, so terribly, painfully, familiar.

Trev's set, unreadable expression was familiar, the waiting room familiar, the cafeteria where they breakfasted during the surgery, familiar. By now little things about Trev were familiar too. He liked his coffee black, bacon crisp, eggs over-easy. He disliked sweet rolls, fake cream and cigarette smoke blown in his face, and he wasn't above freezing a smoker with an icy glare until the offending cigarette was put out.

The operating surgeon had a second surgery scheduled immediately after Mrs. Barrone's and could not talk to them. The assisting doctor, Dr. Helgeson, stopped by to say noncommittally that everything went as well as could be expected. Mrs. Barrone was in the recovery room and it would be several hours before they could see her.

Trev suggested that Robyn might as well go home, but she refused, of course. They waited, the hours dragging by. Late in the afternoon Dr. Martin finally came around. He had just been to check on Mrs. Barrone. He had big, almost beefy hands, Robyn noted irrelevantly. It was difficult to imagine him doing delicate surgery. His manner today was quite different from their earlier meeting with him. He was smiling, cheerful. No, more incredulous than cheerful, Robyn thought.

"She's doing fine," he said, shaking his head unbelievingly. "By all rights, she shouldn't be. At her age and in her condition, what with the stroke and the fracture, to say nothing of the chronic arthritic condition she's suffered for years . . . It's almost unbelievable."

"She's a pretty tough old girl," Trev said. He sounded proud.

The doctor looked at Robyn. "Let's see, you must be Robyn, right?" He looked back at Trev. "And I understand the two of you are going to be married soon. Congratulations."

"How did you know that?" Robyn gasped.

"Mrs. Barrone was quite talkative just before she went under the anesthetic." He laughed. "I think she's more interested in the wedding than her surgery."

"Is she going to recover?" Robyn asked. "I mean, really recover so she can go home before long?"

The doctor's blue eyes turned thoughtful. "I can't guarantee that, of course. As a matter of fact, it's rather difficult, medically speaking, to explain her surprising progress so far. She came through the surgery far better than I expected. And yet I've seen this happen before. For some specific reason a person will set sights on living and against all odds somehow manage to do it. Sometimes when a patient has something special to live for, somehow she just does it, no matter what. I think that is what has happened to Mrs. Barrone. She's so happy about your forthcoming marriage. I gather it is a fairly recent decision?" He looked inquiringly at Robyn.

"Yes, fairly recent," Robyn murmured, her eyes sliding away uneasily.

The doctor stood up. "Well, it's better than any medicine I could give her, that's for certain." He thrust a hand at Trev. "Congratulations again. You're a very lucky man."

"A wedding — takes time," Robyn faltered. "Do you really think — I mean, will she really live to see it?"

"She seems determined to." The doctor paused. "But if you really want her to be there . . . Well, I wouldn't wait too long."

Robyn and Trev stood at the window watching the doctor stride down the hall. Trev's lips were compressed, his expression remote.

As once before, Robyn said uneasily, "Now what?"

Trev's voice was dry. "I think we'd better start planning a wedding."

"A wedding!" Robyn gasped.

With grim determination Trev persisted, "It can be arranged."

Chapter Six

They saw Mrs. Barrone for a few minutes later that day, and Robyn usually drove over for an evening visit after that. She had been neglecting business in her gift shop and she suddenly realized that she had actually failed to open the shop one weekend. Mrs. Barrone made uneven progress, which Robyn found discouraging, though the doctor continually expressed wonder that she was making progress at all. Robyn usually let Trev answer Mrs. Barrone's inquiries about the "wedding." He kept the hospital room bright and fragrant with fresh flowers and always had amusing anecdotes about little incidents around the hospital to lift her spirits.

By now it was all over Caverna Bay that Robyn was officially engaged to Trev. The hardest part for Robyn had been telling Larry. He was shocked, almost stunned. She longed to confide in him, but that was impossible. Robyn found herself always tense, her nerves brittle. The more she was around Trev, the more confused she felt. She had never met a man who made such an impact on her. His pretense of affection in Mrs. Barrone's presence was pure agony for her, and yet she found herself living for those moments, dreading the caress of his hand on her arm or waist and yet yearning for it too. And sometimes, in a kind of horrified fascination, she found her fantasies taking those caresses further. . . .

Why did he do it? she sometimes wondered in frustration and fury. She knew it wasn't only for Mrs. Barrone's benefit because sometimes when Mrs. Barrone couldn't see what he was doing, he caressed the nape of her neck beneath her hair or brushed his fingertips tantalizingly across her skin. Probably, she thought angrily, he did it because he knew exactly how it affected her, knew she was powerless to object, and somehow he found that amusing.

On one Friday evening Robyn arrived at the hospital a little later than usual. The battery in her car had unexpectedly gone dead and she'd had to call the service station for help. When she walked into the hospital room, Trev rose to greet her with his usual kiss on the cheek. She hated the phoniness of his display of affection and yet the touch left her trembling.

Tonight she brushed on by him as quickly as possible, not letting herself look into those amused, mocking eyes. "You look marvelous," she said gaily to Mrs. Barrone, planting a kiss on the faded cheek.

"You don't," Mrs. Barrone observed tartly.

"Oh come now, Grandma, she's the prettiest girl in town and you know it," Trev said reprovingly.

"Beautiful, yes," Mrs. Barrone agreed, eyeing Robyn critically. Her speech was almost back to normal now. "But — peaked. And I think I know why. It's these wedding plans. There's something wrong here."

Robyn felt a sinking rush of dismay. Mrs. Barrone knew! Somehow she had found out that this was all just a terrible pretense.

Robyn took a deep breath. "I'm so sorry —"

"Nothing for you to be sorry about," Mrs. Barrone said briskly. "It's just that I know you too well. You've always had your heart set on a church wedding, haven't you?"

Robyn's lips parted in astonishment. Yes, that was true. She had always pictured her wedding, her *real* wedding, taking place in the sacred setting of a church. She truly believed marriage was forever and a church had always seemed the only proper place to take such vows. But that had nothing to do with this farce!

"Oh, no, I'm delighted with our plans to

be married here in your room," Robyn said hastily.

"No, you aren't, or you wouldn't be looking as droopy as a sick plant." Mrs. Barrone's eyes darted to Trev. "Isn't that true, Trev?"

Trev shrugged and murmured something noncommittal.

"In fact — I have a fuzzy memory of you describing the wedding to me — something about baskets of flowers and a white dress and organ music," Mrs. Barrone continued dreamily.

With rueful amazement Robyn realized Mrs. Barrone's sharp mind had somehow picked up and retained, and perhaps even enlarged, those ridiculous babblings of hers. She looked to Trev for help but he was absentmindedly twisting a vase of roses with one hand and staring off into space. A little desperately Robyn turned back to Mrs. Barrone. "Really, I don't mind having it here."

"No, I insist," Mrs. Barrone said, "you have your church wedding."

Robyn felt a conflicting surge of thoughts and emotions. One part was relief. They wouldn't have to go through some ridiculous phony ceremony here in the room. They would simply have to tell her the truth now. Well, maybe not the whole truth,

Robyn amended as she looked at Mrs. Barrone's lined but bright and eager face.

With sudden inspiration Robyn said, "We couldn't possibly have a church wedding without you, so we'll just postpone it for a while." There, that would keep Mrs. Barrone's spirits up, and then they could just gradually let the "engagement" drift away.

But Mrs. Barrone was having none of that. "Oh no," she said firmly. She distastefully eyed the bulky lump of her bandaged body and leg. "I don't care what these silly doctors say. You make the plans and I'll be there. I'll make it to your wedding if — if it kills me!" she finished a little breathlessly.

Robyn looked helplessly at Trev again, but his face was inscrutable. Mrs. Barrone looked at him expectantly.

"Whatever Robyn wants is fine with me," he murmured.

Robyn's lips tightened angrily. He was unfairly putting the burden of all this on her! "We'll have to think about this," she finally managed to say. "It's quite a change in plans."

"You do it up right," Mrs. Barrone said. "Church, reception, the whole thing. And I'll be there. You can count on it."

Robyn rose to go but Trev made no move to leave. Robyn walked around and deliberately tucked her hand under his elbow.

"Come on, darling," she said sweetly. It was the first time she had used one of his phony terms of endearment. "We have a lot of things to talk about."

They both kissed Mrs. Barrone good-bye. At least *that* affection wasn't counterfeit, Robyn thought. She waited until they were down the hall and well out of Mrs. Barrone's range of hearing before she spoke.

"Obviously the time has come to tell her the truth," Robyn snapped, angry at the lack of help he had given her in Mrs. Barrone's presence.

"The truth?" he repeated with a lift of dark eyebrows. "That we've been lying all along? That we made up the whole story just for her benefit?"

Robyn bit her lip. Suddenly she realized she still had her hand under Trev's arm. She jerked it away. Finally she said evasively, "We wouldn't have to be that blunt. We could just tell her the engagement was off, that we've decided we aren't right for each other. We could make it plain that it didn't affect how either of us felt about *her.*"

Trev said nothing. They brushed by a knot of worried looking people in the main lobby and Trev pulled the heavy outside door open, his face impassive. Outside a light rain was falling.

"Are you listening to what I'm saying?" Robyn cried, frustrated by his silence. "We have to do *something!* We surely can't fake a church wedding."

He stopped and looked down at her squarely. "Then we'll have to have a real one," he said stonily.

"You're out of your mind!" Robyn gasped. "There's no way we can have a 'real' wedding. We must tell her something. She's better now, stronger —"

"Yes, she is," Trev agreed. "Are you going to be the one to destroy the progress she's made? Tell her it was all a lie and break her heart and kill her?"

"I told you, we could be more — tactful than that."

"And break her heart one piece at a time instead of with one big blow? If you can do it, go ahead. But I can't," he said flatly.

"Oh, come on," she scoffed contemptuously. "You fought and loved your way through how many miles of jungle and you can't —"

"I can't."

"You mean you won't!"

He shrugged. "What difference does it make?"

Yes indeed, what difference did it make, Robyn agreed angrily. In either case, it was obvious he did not intend to do anything. If Mrs. Barrone was going to be told anything, truth or half-truth, Robyn herself would have to do the telling.

"That isn't fair," Robyn complained bitterly. They had reached the cars parked side by side now, his sleek Ferrari, her second-hand compact. "I should never have listened to this crazy idea in the first place."

He laughed humorlessly. "Do you think it's something I'd have suggested if you hadn't yelled at me about giving my grandmother something of myself? You seemed to have a rather low opinion of the things I'd tried to do for her. As I recall, my gift of a microwave oven came in for particular criticism."

That was true, Robyn thought unhappily, feeling a slow tide of color flood her face. She was as much to blame as he was for the tangle they were in. And yet they had to do something. They were getting in deeper all the time, like a trap that was slowly but inevitably closing around them, and they were powerless to escape.

Robyn tried again. "But you can't mean that you are willing — that you intend to go through with this. I mean, we are talking now about a real wedding, a *marriage*." Her tongue seemed to twist helplessly around the words.

"Real marriages come to an end too," he said harshly. "The end just comes sooner for some than others."

Yes, of course, Robyn thought slowly. A legal wedding, a quickie divorce later after Mrs. Barrone's death. For all practical purposes the ceremony would be as phony as the one they had planned to stage in Mrs. Barrone's room. It would be more complicated, of course, and there would be the messy details of divorce or annulment afterward. But it still wouldn't be *real*.

And so, almost dazed, Robyn found herself caught up in a small whirlwind of wedding preparations. Trev grimly said that cost didn't matter; he'd pay for everything. She shopped in Eureka for a wedding dress. She shopped around for a new dress for Mrs. Barrone to wear too, spending lots of time describing the dresses she had seen to that delighted elderly woman. They talked about whom to invite to the wedding, what music the organist should play and what kind of cake to order for the reception.

Robyn was gratified to see how happy all this made Mrs. Barrone. She was always cheerful, always in good spirits. She was determined to be able to attend the wedding, and by now Robyn had no doubts but that she would make it.

Robyn hedged as long as possible on actually setting a date for the wedding, but finally it got to the point where nothing more could be done unless a specific date was set. They chose a Friday afternoon at two o'clock. That would mean Mrs. Barrone's elderly friends could attend and still get home before dark. Robyn asked Beth Hylder, a childhood friend, to be her one attendant. For best man, Trev chose Dr. Helgeson, whom he had gotten fairly well acquainted with around the hospital.

A wise choice, Robyn had thought wryly. With not only Mrs. Barrone but also all her elderly friends around, a doctor might very well come in handy. The implication in the fact that Trev did not call on some old friend to be best man was not lost on Robyn, however. Nor were any of his family or friends coming. He had simply shrugged when Robyn asked if there was anyone he wanted to invite. Robyn suspected that except as a local event, the whole marriage and divorce would be very hush-hush, definitely not something he'd care to have publicized.

In spite of all the preparations none of it seemed quite real to Robyn. Even getting the blood tests and license were just more playacting. And yet always in the back of her mind, and sometimes rising to the surface at strange, discomfiting moments, was that odd thought: What if this were all for real? What if it weren't just a carefully staged scene, phony as a movie set? What if when they said, "I do," they really meant they were pledging themselves to each other? And even deeper in Robyn's mind was another thought, a more disturbing one, a thought she dare not face. Something she must keep hidden even from herself.

There was one especially painful, awkward moment. That was when she almost apologetically asked Larry to give her away at the wedding. He agreed, of course. Probably he was too stunned to say no, she thought guiltily. Then he asked a question: What were their plans for after the wedding? Robyn could only answer evasively, murmuring vaguely about Mrs. Barrone's condition and some projects Trev had in mind. Mrs. Barrone hadn't asked about plans, and that future was something Robyn had blacked out of her mind, a bridge to cross when they came to it. Sometimes she had the uneasy feeling Trev intended to spring some unpleasant surprise on her, but he was withdrawn and silent on the few occasions they were alone.

The Friday arrived. Robyn woke with a tense knot already formed in her stomach.

For a moment she couldn't remember why. Then it hit her. This was her wedding day. The happiest day of a girl's life, she thought ironically, and she was loath even to get out of bed.

What was Trev thinking this morning? No doubt wishing, as she was, that he had never gotten tangled up in this mess. And yet, in spite of herself, she felt a tingle of excitement. No one but she and Trev knew this wasn't a *real* wedding. Everyone thought they were in love. And why wouldn't they think that? Robyn thought, half-angrily. Trev certainly gave a convincing performance whenever they were around anyone.

If only that pretense didn't affect her so, she thought, anger directed at herself now. If only the touch of his hand didn't make her tremble, the feel of his lean body send a wild shiver of excitement through her, the look of his smouldering eyes ignite a flame somewhere deep within her. It was crazy. He was doing no more than acting. They should have starred him in his own movie, she thought contemptuously. And yet . . .

By tonight it would all be over and she would be back here in her own bed. All she had to do was somehow get through the day.

She forced herself to down toast and coffee for breakfast. She spent the morning having her hair done at Caverna Bay's lone beauty shop. She took her wedding gown over to the little room off the main church, where she would dress. She was surprised to find the florists already there decorating the church with what appeared to be at least a truckload of flowers. She couldn't manage lunch. It simply would not go down.

At one o'clock Larry came by to pick her up and take her to the church. He was already dressed for his part in the ceremony. He had an odd look on his face as he reached over to squeeze her hand. "I hope you'll be happy. I really do," he said huskily.

"Thank you, Larry. You've been so good to me. I don't know what I'd have done without you." Impulsively she leaned over and kissed him on the cheek.

"I always wanted to go through a marriage ceremony with you, but I never pictured it being quite like this. I guess sometimes our dreams come true, but in the wrong way." Then he gave her a funny little crooked grin and apologized. "I'm sorry. I shouldn't be upsetting you by saying things like this. If you're happy — well, that's the important thing."

She smiled her thanks, tears glistening on her lashes.

"Ready to tell me your plans yet?" Larry

inquired lightly. When she didn't answer, he smiled again. "Okay, I get the picture. I suppose Trev is trying to avoid publicity. But I can't help feeling — Do you love the guy?" he asked suddenly with a blunt directness she could not ignore. "Really love him?"

Robyn paused with her hand on the door handle. There it was, she thought, the question she had not dared ask herself. She had skirted it by contemptuously berating herself for her susceptibility to Trev's physical charms. She had told herself the very idea of being in love with him was totally unthinkable, unworthy of serious consideration. But now she couldn't avoid the question any longer. Larry wouldn't let her.

She took a deep breath. "Yes. Yes, I really love him." She intended the words to come out firm but she could hear the tremble in her own voice.

Larry heard something more. "You don't sound very happy about it," he observed.

What was it Larry had said just a few moments ago? "Sometimes our dreams come true, but in the wrong way." Yes, here it was, her dream come true. She was deeply, desperately in love. She was marrying the man she loved. And yet it was all terribly, hopelessly wrong, like some misshapen distortion in a trick mirror. She pressed her trembling lips together, struggling for control.

"I'm h— happy," she finally managed to falter. "Just bridal jitters. You know."

Larry looked as if he was about to dispute that, but just then Beth Hylder stuck her head out the rear door of the church. "You'd better get dressed," she called. "The bridegroom is threatening to start the ceremony without you."

Robyn's heart flip-flopped. Trev was already here. And already issuing orders and ultimatums too, she thought resentfully. Larry gave her hand another encouraging squeeze and then she slipped out of the car. There was no time for second thoughts now.

Robyn dressed swiftly. The ivory satin felt cool and rich against her skin. The fitted bodice molded her slim waist and breasts, and the flowing skirt swirled around her legs. Beth fluttered around her, adjusting a seam here, a bit of lace there.

The tight knot in Robyn's stomach was a churning sea of nausea now. One part of her was protesting that she couldn't go through with this travesty; another part was reminding her that for Mrs. Barrone's sake she had to go through with it. Beth kept dashing back and forth, peeking out the window to see who was arriving. Suddenly she announced the arrival of a photographer.

"From Beckley's Studio in Eureka," she added, sounding impressed. "They cost a fortune."

Photographer? Surely Beth must be mistaken, Robyn thought. She hadn't arranged for any photographs. Why would Trev want any record of this day?

Robyn slipped on the white satin shoes. She hadn't bothered fulfilling the "Something old, something new, something borrowed, something blue" tradition, and suddenly Beth noticed, horrified, that there was nothing blue. Hastily she ran out to see what she could find.

Robyn was standing in front of the mirror trying to arrange her hair around the tiara of seed pearls holding the lace and net veil when there was a tap on the door.

"Who is it?" she called.

"Trev."

Robyn's hands suddenly froze on the tiara. She looked at herself in the mirror. Her eyes stared back, unnaturally large and dark, her skin pale in spite of carefully applied makeup. Her lower lip trembled and she reached up a shaky hand to touch it, suddenly thinking irrelevantly that in a few minutes Trev would kiss those trembling lips. She swallowed convulsively.

"Robyn? Are you all right?" The voice was

sharper now. "I'd like to talk to you for a minute."

Resolutely she walked over and pulled the door open. "Yes? What is it you want?" She managed to keep her voice crisp and businesslike.

He stepped inside and pulled the door shut behind him. His eyes swept over her. Approval? Indifference? She could not tell. Strange emotions ricocheted through Robyn. She looked away and fingered the pointed tip of her fitted satin sleeve. His intense, blue gaze unnerved her, and she struggled to regain her composure. She forced herself to inspect him coolly, trying not to be swayed by his dark good looks.

"Does that searching gaze mean that I pass muster, or are you thinking that the bridegroom isn't supposed to see the bride before the ceremony?" he asked.

"Under the circumstances I don't think that really matters," Robyn returned evenly. But she still could not meet his look. She knew the devastating effect those smouldering eyes had on her. She turned back to the mirror and fussed nervously with the tiara.

"You said you wanted to talk to me," she prompted. "There isn't much time."

"Maybe I just wanted to make sure you

were going through with this. That I wasn't going to be left standing at the altar with a ring in my hand and a foolish expression on my face," he said.

"I'm sure you know I wouldn't do anything to hurt Mrs. Barrone," Robyn said aloofly.

In the mirror, Robyn saw the lift of a dark eyebrow. "But what if she were not even involved?"

"If she wasn't involved, we wouldn't be in this mess," Robyn pointed out. Suddenly her composure broke and she turned away from his reflection in the mirror. "Trev, what we're doing is a farce! A travesty! All those decent people out there and we're making fools out of them. And we're the biggest fools of all!" she cried.

He looked at her a moment longer and then shrugged. He pulled a packet of papers out of a breast pocket. "I'd like you to read this. My lawyer drew it up."

The stiff pages crackled as Robyn unfolded them slowly. "What is it?"

"A prenuptial agreement. It says if we come to a — ah — parting of the ways that we each retain whatever property or possessions we brought to the marriage and make no claim on the other person's properties."

Robyn glanced up, surprised and angry.

"Did you really think I might try to benefit from this sorry mess?" she asked bitterly.

"It protects you as well as me," he pointed out. "You don't have to worry that I might try to claim an interest in your gift shop."

"How considerate of you," she returned sarcastically.

He held out a pen and she scratched her signature on the document.

"Don't you want to read the agreement?"

"I'm sure your lawyer is thoroughly competent," she snapped. "Now, if you'll leave me alone, I'd like to finish dressing." She turned her back on him again and fumbled with the veil, determinedly ignoring him.

After a moment she heard the door open and watched in the mirror as he walked out.

She closed the door with shaking hands and leaned against it. She felt dizzy. Prenuptial agreements . . . Beth earnestly borrowing something blue for her to fulfill the old wedding tradition . . . the awful agony of finally admitting to herself she was in love with Trev. It was all such a confused jumble. Her head throbbed. She could not go through with this. She simply could not do it.

Suppose she just ran out the back way and disappeared, she thought wildly. It wouldn't be the first time a bride had changed her mind at the last minute.

Then, as she was peering out the window, a car pulled up. Dr. Helgeson and a nurse and Mrs. Barrone arriving. Little Mrs. Barrone was sitting up very straight. She had made it! She was going to see her beloved grandson married to a "nice, sensible young lady," as she had always hoped.

Robyn turned away from the window. Nice, sensible young ladies did not run out on their responsibilities and commitments. She shuddered to think of the consequences to Mrs. Barrone if she gave in to such a wild impulse. As she had told Trev, she couldn't do anything to hurt Mrs. Barrone. And neither, she thought with a sense of wonder, could he. In spite of her accusation about his inability to feel love, she knew it wasn't true. He was as trapped as Robyn by his feelings for that sweet old lady.

Trapped, but not so blind that he wasn't looking ahead and making careful plans for the future, Robyn reminded herself with distaste. He did not intend to be caught unprepared when all this finally came to an end.

That was what she must concentrate on too, she thought determinedly. All she had to do today was get through this afternoon. The ceremony and reception together couldn't possibly last more than a couple of hours. If she could just hold herself together that long, the worst would be over. Mrs. Barrone would go back to her hospital room. Trev would go to his motel. And she could go back to her own safe little apartment behind the gift shop. And then it was just a matter of time. In spite of Mrs. Barrone's determined progress, none of the doctors held out much hope for a permanent recovery.

And that was where Robyn's thoughts and emotions became confused between hope and guilt. She desperately wanted all this to be over and yet she didn't want Mrs. Barrone to die, and one couldn't happen without the other. The throbbing pain was back in Robyn's head again. If only she hadn't fallen in love with Trev, she thought dully. That was what complicated everything, made her mind and body go all soft and helpless when he touched her, made her ache with pain when she thought of the hopelessness of her feelings for him. If she could only look at all this as he did, a nuisance and a bother, but justified for Mrs. Barrone's sake. . . .

A tap on the door. "Robyn?" Beth said tentatively. "Everything is ready."

"I'm coming."

Robyn took another quick look in the mirror. Veil in place, troubled eyes safely concealed. Dress falling in perfect, elegant folds to the floor. Engagement ring gleaming on her right hand, left hand bare to receive the wedding band. She realized she was still clutching the blue lace handkerchief Beth had given her. Shakily she tucked it inside the bodice of her gown. She picked up her bouquet of cream colored roses, and opened the door to face the strange torment of marrying the man she loved.

After that everything was a blur oddly punctuated by sharp moments of startling clarity, like a film run at high speed stopping occasionally for a still. The blur of a church filled with masses of flowers and a small sea of unidentifiable faces. The blur of music. Larry supporting her on his arm. Heady fragrance of flowers. Finally, a still, clear shot of Mrs. Barrone in a wheelchair at the edge of the front pew, her face radiant with happiness.

Then Trev and Robyn were standing before the altar. The minister spoke. Robyn and Trev repeated the words as he had told them to do. Trev slipped the ring on her finger. More words from the minister. To Robyn, they sounded dim and far away. Was all this really happening to her?

Someone lifted the veil from her face and she looked up to meet Trev's deep, unfathomable eyes.

Moving toward her, he swept her into his arms. He lifted his hand to touch her cheek and throat with wondering gentleness before sliding it caressingly down her smooth, satin back now arching willingly toward him. As in slow motion, she saw his face move down to meet hers as she parted her lips to accept his kiss. For the first time she found out what it was like to be kissed by Trevor Barrone. Not the brush of lips on cheek or temple, but a passionate kiss. The kiss of a man who desired a woman and was going to make sure that she knew it.

Finally he let her go. Her mouth felt seared and bruised. Waves of heat coursed through her body. She felt nude — exposed — it was unseemly in front of everyone. And yet — and yet — she yearned with all her heart and soul to be in Trevor Barrone's arms again.

She was still trembling when the organist began the strains of the triumphal march. Trevor tucked her arm in his. Beneath the satin of her long sleeve she could feel her flesh respond to his possessive grip. They marched down the aisle amid a sea of faces. A flash bulb popped. Mr. and Mrs. Trevor Barrone had been recorded for posterity.

The reception was held in a separate wing of the church. Mrs. Barrone's elderly friends turned out to be surprisingly energetic, and everything was bright and festive. Trev and Robyn joined hands to cut the three-tiered cake with the little bride and groom figures on top. More photographs, several with Mrs. Barrone beaming proudly. Robyn realized now why Trev had hired a photographer. For Mrs. Barrone, of course. She would wear the photographs ragged enjoying them herself and showing them off.

Trev was at his best, treating Mrs. Barrone and all her friends gallantly, making a display of attentive affection toward Robyn. But for Robyn it was more difficult. She had to open the wedding gifts. It didn't seem right to her that so many had taken of their limited resources to buy gifts for a wedding couple who were total frauds. Robyn tried to make up for her guilt by oohing and aahing enthusiastically over each item, from handmade potholders to lovely crocheted tablecloths.

By now her mouth ached from smiling so widely. The satin shoes hurt her feet. She couldn't hang on much longer. And, she realized, Mrs. Barrone was tiring fast. Robyn shot an appealing glance at Trev. Couldn't they get this over with?

He raised a hand. "Before everyone leaves —"

Nicely put, Robyn thought wryly. A gentle hint to say the least.

"Before everyone leaves, I have an announcement to make."

Robyn was standing beside Mrs. Barrone's wheelchair. She felt a sudden twinge of uneasiness as Trev threw her an odd, almost challenging glance. Announcement about what?

"I'm sure you've all been wondering about our plans, and I apologize for being so secretive. It's just that I wanted to surprise everyone, including my lovely bride." He flashed a brilliant smile in Robyn's direction. "As some of you may know, I had planned to move my grandmother down to the southern part of the state with me. She was not, to say the least, wildly enthusiastic about the idea."

A small wave of laughter tittered through the attentive crowd. Robyn felt a wave of apprehension. What in the world was he getting at?

"So I decided to change my plans," Trevor continued. "I have bought a house in Caverna Bay where I spent so many summers with my grandmother and where I met my beautiful bride."

Trevor smiled lovingly at Robyn who was too bewildered to smile back.

"Some of you probably know the house — it's the new, modern one overlooking the bay."

Robyn gasped audibly. It was the house on Rocky Point. The one she had thought belonged to a television personality.

Trevor walked over to Robyn and took her hand. "My grandmother already knew about this; we had to make the arrangements but, by the look on her face, I would say that this came as a complete surprise to my bride, wouldn't you?"

Everyone crowded around Trev and Robyn. Robyn answered questions and congratulations alike with the same automatic smile. But inside, she was shaking. She had been trapped again! Her ordeal was not yet over. Not only would she have to continue this ridiculous deception, but she would have to live in the same house with the man who had been responsible for it. And who knew where that would lead? She stole a look at Trevor but he seemed to be completely absorbed in conversation with his guests.

Chapter Seven

They left the church in a flurry of rice and flashbulbs. A procession of honking cars followed. Robyn leaned back against the seat, eyes closed, angry with Trev for the "surprise" he had pulled on her but too drained at the moment to protest. Now was when it should have been all over. But it wasn't — it wasn't! The worst was only beginning. Being around Trev all the time, living a 24-hour-a-day pretense. How could he do this to her? How *dare* he do it without even consulting her, springing it on her at a time when he knew she couldn't protest?

She had wondered several times why Mrs. Barrone never questioned them about their plans for after the wedding. But now she knew the reason. Mrs. Barrone already knew the plans. Only Robyn had been in the dark.

Robyn opened her eyes and glanced over at Trev. Once away from the church the flashing smile had disappeared. He looked at Robyn, then back at the winding road that led around the south side of the bay.

"Most brides would be delighted to be

surprised with a beautiful new home on their wedding day," he said mockingly.

Robyn opened her mouth to make a withering retort and then compressed her lips angrily. This was neither the time nor place for all she had to say. The honking cars made speech practically impossible.

Trev turned off the main road at a pair of high, gracefully peaked, wrought iron gates. They followed the driveway through a forest of towering redwoods. The house was awe inspiring, a huge structure of angled rooftops, decks, massive stone and wide expanses of glass. The landscaping was an elegant blend of trees and shrubs and artfully placed rocks designed to blend with the natural setting. Trev braked in front of the recessed entryway. Robyn reluctantly slid out. She was still in her wedding gown. Trev was looking at her with an oddly expectant expression.

"It's lovely," Robyn murmured almost unwillingly. "I'm sure your grandmother will love it."

In the distance she could still hear the tooting horns as the cars circled back toward town. Robyn turned to look through the massive tree trunks at the little town across the bay. Suddenly she was swept off her feet into Trev's strong arms. She looked up into his blue eyes with astonishment. "What are you doing?" she gasped.

"Carrying my bride across the threshold."

Robyn felt a wild surge of excitement. His face was only inches from hers, her body pressed almost painfully against his chest. Deftly, he opened the heavy door without loosening his grip on her. The satin of her dress was a seductive barrier between his hands and her skin. Her dress caught on the door, slipping up to expose a slim and shapely thigh. Trev slid the dress down but she felt his gaze and touch lingering on her exposed leg.

Robyn felt her breath catch and hold. They were alone. No need for pretense now. Yet he was looking at her with a strangely raw, hungry look.

And then Dr. Helgeson's car slid neatly to a stop behind the Ferrari. Robyn's excitement drained away. Of course, Trev was only preparing a pleasant little scene for Mrs. Barrone to see when she arrived, the happy groom carrying the blushing bride over the threshold. Trev never missed a trick.

Robyn held her body stiff and unyielding as Trev carried her inside. "You can put me down," she snapped as soon as they were out of Mrs. Barrone's sight. "No one can see us now so you can drop the act."

Still he didn't release her. His eyes narrowed appraisingly. "You think everything I do is an act for someone else's benefit?"

Without waiting for an answer he whirled and carried her up the open stairway to a balcony of rooms overlooking the huge living room. Robyn pounded on his chest, frightened by his determined expression. He flung her across the bed. She barely had time to utter an enraged protest before his body trapped hers on the bed, holding her breathless beneath him.

"Let me — go!" she gasped.

If he heard, he made no sign. His eyes were half closed as he covered her eyes and temples and throat with kisses. Robyn struggled to free herself, but his lips found hers, and, against her will, she found her body responding. His body moved against hers, one hand slipping beneath her back to mold her body against his, his mouth devouring hers hungrily in a kiss that sent her senses spinning dizzily.

When he finally lifted his mouth from hers, their eyes met, Robyn's astonished, his, darkened by passion. Slowly he stood up and ran a hand through his hair, pushing back the strands that had fallen across his forehead. He straightened his tie, his eyes still never breaking their hold on hers.

Robyn hadn't moved. He leaned over her, one hand on either side of her. "Was that an act?" he demanded harshly.

"I — I don't know what you mean!" she gasped.

He looked at her a moment longer before saying enigmatically, "No, perhaps you don't."

He straightened, his manner once more formally polite. "I think you'll find everything you need in the closet and bathroom. I had Luther go to your place and bring your things over during the ceremony." Then, with another of those flashing smiles, he was gone, leaving Robyn to raise a trembling hand to her bruised mouth.

She was numb, unable to move. Her glance roamed slowly around the huge bedroom, more elegant than anything she had ever seen. Gleaming, richly-hued furnishings, pale ivory carpeting, built-in bar, television and stereo. The bedspread beneath her was puffed patchwork velvet, soft and luxuriously sensuous. Sliding glass doors opened onto a private deck. Slowly she got up and went to a walk-in closet. Her clothes were there, neatly hanging on one rod, much space still bare. The bathroom was larger than her entire bedroom back home, her startled gaze was reflected in a series of angled mirrors. She ran a hand over the luxurious dressing table; her small supply of toiletries looked dwarfed in this elegance.

And then a shocking thought hit her. She raced to the other closet and flung the door open. It was half full of suits, neatly hanging pants, shirts, shoes, boots.

Trev thought — expected — how dare he!

Robyn grabbed a beige jersey blouse and brown pants from her closet and stormed into the bathroom to change, hastily locking the door behind her. Her hands trembled as she pulled the slithery blouse around her shoulders, trembled with fury and a kind of incriminating weakness that she found almost terrifying. If Trev hadn't stopped on his own . . .

Determinedly she decided she must make one thing plain to Trev at once. There was a point beyond which she would not carry this charade. She marched into the closet to gather up an armload of her clothes and move them elsewhere, but then she hesitated. It would look a little strange if she ran into Dr. Helgeson or the nurse while carting her belongings. Reluctantly she replaced the clothing in the closet.

She hurried down the stairs. No one seemed to be around. Then she spotted an open door down a hallway. There she found Mrs. Barrone in her wheelchair admiring the pleasant little patio with a backdrop of redwoods just outside more sliding glass doors. Robyn was astonished to see that the room was already lavishly equipped with a hospital bed, a television conveniently suspended so it could be watched from the bed, plus Mrs. Barrone's familiar plants scattered everywhere, with no need for rotation in this light, airy room.

"Robyn! There you are. Trev said you'd gone up to change."

"Where is he?"

"Dr. Helgeson was having a problem with his car. He and Trev went to look at it. Mrs. Bundy went to get her things out of the car."

"She's going to be your private nurse?"

"No. Trev has hired someone else. I understand she hasn't arrived yet, so Mrs. Bundy agreed to stay for a day or two." She held out her hand to Robyn, her faded eyes suddenly glistening. "You don't know how happy you've made me."

"I'm happy too." The words came out automatically. Robyn squeezed the frail hand.

"But I feel terrible about intruding on the two of you like this. I know it's because of me you're not even taking a honeymoon."

"No, really, that isn't it."

"You should at least have had a couple of weeks to yourselves here in the house before I came," Mrs. Barrone fussed. "The last thing a pair of young lovers needs is an old lady and some busybody nurse bustling around. The two of you deserve some time alone together."

Robyn had a sudden vision of just Trev and herself here in the house together. No interruptions, just a romantic fire in the fireplace, the lights of the bay below, the tempting, velvet-covered bed upstairs . . . Her palms felt damp and that strange feeling of giddy weakness swept over her as she remembered the feel of Trev's strong, hard body holding her down. The danger inherent in such a situation sent a shiver throughout her body.

"I'm glad you're here," Robyn said, trying to control the tremulousness in her voice. "Very glad," she added almost vehemently, struggling to blot out that half-frightening, half-tantalizing vision.

"Do you like the house?" Mrs. Barrone asked.

"Yes, it's lovely." Robyn strolled over to the sliding glass door and looked out at the redwoods. "You knew about the house?" she asked tentatively.

"Yes. Trev realized that I would never leave

Caverna Bay, and that's why he was away when I fell. He had gone down to Los Angeles to see about selling the house near Palm Springs and buying this one. I'm a terrible bother, I guess." She smiled mischievously. "But considering the way things worked out, I can't say I'm sorry."

So this house was the "business" that had taken Trev out of town, Robyn realized in surprise. Why had he never told her? It would certainly have justified his absence. But Trev, she thought scornfully, would never feel obligated to justify any of his actions.

"Trev asked me not to tell you," Mrs. Barrone added. "He wanted to surprise you."

The understatement of the year, Robyn thought grimly. Aloud she said hesitantly, "Did our marriage surprise you?"

"Not really," Mrs. Barrone returned. "You made quite an impression on Trev that day you met on the beach, you know. He came home and asked me a million questions about you."

"He did?" Robyn asked, flustered both by the surprising information and Mrs. Barrone's knowing nod. She changed the subject. "This is such a magnificent place. I wonder — I mean, I know Trev made a lot of

173

money from the book and movie, but —"

"But you're wondering if he can afford all this." Mrs. Barrone laughed. "I don't think you have to worry. Trev's other grandparents were quite wealthy and he inherited a great deal from them. Then he also inherited his mother's property when she died of a rare kidney disease while he was in Africa."

Surprised again, Robyn turned away from the view of the redwoods. "I didn't know that she was dead."

"I didn't either." Mrs. Barrone's lined face looked suddenly sad. "I feel guilty now. All those bad thoughts I had about her for so many years. From what Trev says, she always knew she might not live very long. Perhaps it explains why she tried to grab everything she could from life while she had the chance."

Robyn strolled restlessly around the room. The grass green carpet with a scattering of cheerful yellow throw rugs and the plants made the room almost an indoor garden. Beyond the gleaming bathroom a door opened onto an adjoining room for a nurse.

"Has Trev ever said anything about why he never contacted you all those years?" Robyn asked.

Mrs. Barrone hesitated a moment before

speaking. "His mother told him — things. She let him think I was a rich, greedy old lady who didn't want anything to do with him because I disapproved of her."

"Why, that's terrible!" Robyn gasped indignantly.

"Perhaps it had something to do with her illness. And perhaps it was my fault too. I should have tried harder to understand her," Mrs. Barrone said with her characteristic charity. It was obvious she intended to hold no grudges for what was past. "But Trev is here now and you two have each other, and that is all that matters. He loves you very much, you know."

"Did he tell you that?" Robyn asked, feeling a strange rush of hope.

"No, but I can tell. And I know you love him deeply too."

Mrs. Bundy bustled back in then, carrying an overnight bag and some flowers she had scooped up from the church. Together she and Robyn helped move Mrs. Barrone into the standard hospital bed. Robyn kissed Mrs. Barrone on the cheek and said she thought she would take a further look around the house.

She wandered back to the living room. Darkness and fog had moved in, blotting out the view. Someone had lit a crackling fire in the fireplace. An enormous, obviously custom-made sofa lined the full length of the windows. A magnificent seascape decorated the wall beneath the overhanging balcony. She sat down on a plush ottoman in front of the fire and crossed her arms on her knees, staring into the flames.

The conversation with Mrs. Barrone had been illuminating. It explained several things: Trev's lack of communication with his grandmother over the years, his out of town business trip which Robyn had been so quick to assume was for less honorable purposes. His concern for his grandmother was evident in the time and effort he had put into preparing her room.

But Robyn had to laugh grimly at herself for the hope that had surged through her when Mrs. Barrone spoke of Trev's "love" for Robyn. If Trev had convinced his grandmother he really loved Robyn, it was yet another tribute to his marvelous acting ability. But Mrs. Barrone was all too correct about Robyn's feelings for Trev, she thought unhappily.

A noise behind her startled her out of her reverie. She had been sitting there so long that the fire had died to glowing coals and the room had grown dark around her.

"I'm sorry. I didn't mean to startle you."

Trev had changed clothes and was now wearing casual slacks and shirt. Robyn eyed him warily.

"Grandma is sleeping and Mrs. Bundy is having supper on a tray in her room. I asked Luther to bring us something light here."

Robyn realized she hadn't eaten anything but a few bites of wedding cake since her skimpy breakfast that morning. "Who is Luther?" Robyn asked.

"He and his wife used to work for my grandparents. Marie is a marvelous cook. We'll probably need someone else to help around the house."

Robyn took a deep breath. It was time to get things straightened out *now*. "Why are my things in your room?" she asked bluntly.

"I imagine because that is where Luther thought they belonged," Trev answered mildly. Pointedly he added, "I do believe I recall a minister pronouncing us husband and wife."

Robyn chewed her lower lip uncertainly. She supposed it was possible the unseen Luther had put her things in Trev's room on the assumption that was where they belonged. And it was also possible that was where Trev had told Luther to put them, and he was even now laughing inwardly at her discomfort. She looked at him out of the corner of her eye. He had dropped to the floor, his back against the sofa, long legs stretched out in front of the fireplace. He looked relaxed, comfortable and at home. A chunk of wood fell, flickering into flames. The flames highlighted his dark hair and made the smile he turned on her almost devilish.

"Penny for your thoughts?" he said lightly.

"My things will have to be moved to another room." She was annoyed that her voice came out sounding prissy instead of authoritative.

"Whatever you say," he agreed, surprisingly genial. "Would you like me to call Luther and have him move them now?"

Robyn hesitated, thinking how odd that would look to the servant. Reluctantly she said, "No, I'll do it myself."

"There's plenty of time," Trev agreed. "At least wait until we eat." He reached over and tossed another chunk of wood on the fire. Silently, they both watched the shower of sparks rise up the chimney.

"Why did you buy this place?" she asked.

"Grandma was adamant that she wouldn't leave Caverna Bay. Then when you wouldn't help convince her —"

"I never said that," Robyn broke in indignantly. "I fully intended to go over and talk to her. I realize now I should have gone sooner, of course, but at the time I was — busy," she finished lamely.

"I waited, and when you didn't show up —"

"You couldn't have waited very long," Robyn protested. Her back suddenly felt stiff and achy from sitting on the ottoman so long. She stood up. Standing made her feel more in control of the situation. "You were just angry because I didn't jump like a trained dog at your command. And when you bought the house, you might at least have told me."

"At first I didn't see any point in it," he said logically. "No one expected her to live."

That was true, Robyn agreed reluctantly. It was the very reason they had gotten into this involved tangle. "But it wasn't fair, springing it on me at the church like that."

"No, I suppose not. But, frankly, I was afraid you wouldn't go through with the wedding if you knew about the house. Would you have?" he challenged.

"I don't know. But I should have had the chance to make up my own mind."

He gave her a warning look and she realized someone was approaching through the shadows. Trev introduced the servant, Luther, who was carrying a large tray of covered dishes.

"Just set the tray over there," Trev directed. "We'll help ourselves."

Luther set the tray on the raised hearth. He was carrying a silver bucket holding a bottle of champagne surrounded by crushed ice. He set the bucket below the hearth, away from the heat of the flames, and departed as quietly as he had come.

Robyn looked at the little scene uneasily, throat suddenly tight. Romantically flickering fire, champagne chilling, Trev relaxed and looking dangerously attractive half-sitting, half-lying by the fire. She walked determinedly toward the big lamp midway down the long sofa. "I'll get the light. It seems rather dark in here."

She shouldn't have walked so close to him. He reached out and trapped her ankle lightly.

"No. Don't. Just the firelight is pleasant, don't you think?" He paused, then went on. "Look, I realize this is all very inconvenient for you, to say the least. And I have to admit it isn't what I had in mind when I first suggested we tell Grandma what I thought was a deathbed story of our getting married. But it's too late now. We're here. We might as well make the best of a bad situation. It is, after all, only temporary, if that's any consolation for you."

It was — and it wasn't, Robyn thought unhappily, the confusion of feelings returning. She didn't want Mrs. Barrone to die. She had no doubt but that this deception had prolonged Mrs. Barrone's life and increased her happiness and peace of mind immeasurably. But until Mrs. Barrone died Robyn was trapped here. And so, of course, was Trev, she reminded herself as she eyed him warily again. He was no doubt right. The thing to do was make the best of the situation. How many chances would she ever have to live in a house like this, with servants and an incredible view — and champagne chilling in a silver bucket? If only she didn't feel about Trev the way she did! If only she could take this as resignedly as he was doing, without the sweet-painful ache of her hopeless love for him.

"Look, it's our wedding night," he said lightly. "Can't we at least be friends?"

His tone was so disarming that Robyn felt confused. He seemed different now, no longer harsh and arrogant, but gentle, even understanding. Sympathetic to her position. Perhaps he had resigned himself to making the best of an awkward situation.

"Friends?" he asked, thrusting out a hand for a handshake.

"Friends," Robyn agreed, returning the

hearty handshake and trying to ignore the thrill even that impersonal touch gave her.

Trev uncovered the dishes. Sitting companionably cross-legged on the floor, they ate delicately flavored crab bisque and crusty French bread topped with a sprinkling of parmesan cheese. There was a plate of crisp relishes and, to Robyn's astonishment, even a large slice of wedding cake complete with two forks.

"I see Marie is a romantic," Trev said dryly. "I wonder where she got hold of that."

"Don't look at me," Robyn retorted.

"Champagne?" he suggested.

"Why not?" Robyn returned recklessly in the same casual, friendly tone. He smiled at her, firelight gleaming in his eyes.

He opened the bottle expertly, producing a satisfactory pop without spilling any of the sparkling liquid. Robyn hesitantly accepted a gracefully curved goblet. She'd never tasted champagne and wasn't sure how she would react to it.

To her surprise the champagne was delicious, light and bubbling. Trev seemed as surprised as she was at how easily she tossed it down. He refilled her glass approvingly.

"Good. It'll relax you. You've been all tied up in knots for days. In fact, you're sitting there all tense and stiff right now, aren't you?"

Robyn protested that she was perfectly relaxed, but he moved around behind her and massaged her back and shoulders. He was right, she thought dreamily as the champagne and the warmth of his moving fingers flowed through her. She *was* tense and stiff. She could feel the tenseness draining away under his skillful hands.

"Will Mrs. Barrone's private nurse arrive soon?" she asked. She sipped another glass of champagne, savoring each sparkling drop.

His fingers worked the taut, sore muscles along her neck and shoulders. "I thought she'd be here by now."

"Who is she? Where is she from?"

"She's coming up from San Francisco." His hands massaged the long muscles on either side of her spine. It felt heavenly and his voice was softly soothing, almost hypnotic. "She's very experienced and competent and capable, just like Mrs. Bundy."

We should talk some more, Robyn thought vaguely. There were so many things to discuss — what she was going to do about the shop until this was all over and how they were going to carry out this crazy charade. But somehow all that seemed very far away and unimportant. Dreamily Robyn realized Trev was no longer just massaging her back and shoulders. His lips trailed a whisper of kisses along the back of her neck. His hands deftly loosened her blouse and exposed a shoulder, creamy in the firelight, to another rain of warm kisses.

A warning rang somewhere far back in her mind. She must stop him, this was going dangerously too far. She could feel a warm weakness seeping through her, a languid feeling that made her soft and yielding to his touch. She tried to protest, but all that came out was a husky, helpless, "Trev —"

He didn't speak. His fingers caressed the hollow of her throat, the line of her jaw, then roamed in wild exploration over her body as she twisted and turned, hardly knowing whether she was trying to escape the exquisite pain of that touch or bring it closer.

"Please — don't —"

His hands caressed the smooth skin beneath the blouse that was now open to her waist. His lips found the gentle swell of her breasts and lingered in the hollow between them. Robyn had the wild feeling that she was being played like some finely-tuned instrument, and yet the music was too sweet to stop and she throbbed to it.

His seeking hand turned her mouth to his and her lips parted of their own accord to meet his. The kiss was deep, probing, passionate. She was only dimly aware when he pushed her back against the lush carpeting, his body half beside, half over hers.

This wasn't real, one part of her said reassuringly. This was just another of her wild fantasies. Another fantasy in which she was free to say and do whatever she pleased. She reached up and touched his face with seeking fingertips, traced the chiseled curve of his lips, ran her hand through his thick hair, pulled his head down to meet her lips again in a wild, abandoned kiss. Her fingers tangled in the dark hair of his chest, and her arched body moved wantonly against his.

"Let's go upstairs," he whispered hoarsely.

For a moment her body went rigid and her eyes wide with shock. This was no fantasy, no dream. This Trev beside her was real, his body lean and hard against hers. When had he removed his shirt so the firelight gleamed on naked, bronzed skin, so his bare skin pressed against hers with only the lacy wisp of her underthings between them? Even now his hands, oddly clumsy with haste, fumbled to remove the barrier.

She must stop him, she thought wildly. Now, before it was too late. But some primitive force within her told her it was already too late, an animal desire seemed to have taken control of her body. Her will, her mind said stop, but this other tumultuous, compelling force made her hands roam over the smooth, bare skin of his back, exulting in the feel of his demanding body straining against hers.

His groping fingers found the obstinate hook. She caught her breath as she felt the release.

The noise shrilled only inches from Robyn's head. For a moment the interruption failed to register as anything more than an annoying noise, and then she realized it was a telephone ringing.

Trev cursed under his breath. "Don't answer it," he muttered. His face was only inches from hers, dark hair tumbled across heavy-lidded eyes. She tried to move and he held her down with his body. "It'll stop in a minute," he said roughly.

But the phone didn't stop. It jangled on and on.

"We'd better answer it," she said uneasily.

"Luther will get it."

That thought made Robyn suddenly struggle to a sitting position. What if Luther answered the phone and then came to tell Trev politely that it was for him — and found Robyn here half undressed, hair disheveled? She grabbed for the ringing phone.

"Yes?" she said breathlessly.

There was a moment of silence, as if the

person on the other end of the line was surprised to hear a female voice.

Then, "May I speak to Trev, please?" The voice was young, feminine, somehow suggestive in saying even that simple line.

"May I ask who is calling?" Robyn said crisply. She didn't know why she asked that. It just popped out.

"Tell him it's Shauna."

"Shauna?" Robyn repeated dumbly. The name went with the seductive voice.

Trev reached for the phone. Robyn handed it to him and then moved away, clutching the drooping blouse around her. She turned her back to him to frantically refasten the hook he had released. Good Lord, what had gotten into her? she wondered, shocked, as she spied her disheveled reflection in the dark windows. She felt as if she had just returned from some dangerous leaping-off point, jerked back just as she was about to fall. Which was a rather accurate description of what had almost happened, she thought breathlessly. She had acted cheap and wanton.

But was making love with someone you loved cheap and wanton? a part of her asked. Another part of her answered: *Yes, when he doesn't love you!*

She stood up and headed for the stairs.

"Wait!" Trev called to Robyn, then laughingly into the phone, "No, not you. We'll see you sometime tomorrow then, okay?" He put the phone down and strode toward Robyn. "Where are you going?"

"Upstairs," she said. "But not to your bedroom, if that's what you're thinking." She hesitated, not wanting to admit curiosity but too curious not to ask. "Who was that?"

"Shauna McNary, the nurse I hired to take care of Grandma. She had car trouble and she's staying overnight down the coast. She'll be here tomorrow." He put a possessive arm around her. "Let's have another glass of champagne," he coaxed.

Earlier Trev had referred to the new nurse as "experienced and capable and competent," somehow giving Robyn the impression she was as middle-aged and dowdy as Mrs. Bundy. That voice on the phone had sounded neither middle-aged nor dowdy, and Robyn suddenly had a different thought about just what sort of "experience" this Shauna might have. She remembered that the woman had asked for "Trev," not "Mr. Barrone" as might be expected of a new employee.

"You know her personally, I take it?" Robyn questioned.

"Yes, more or less," Trev acknowledged impatiently. "I was hospitalized in San Francisco after I came back from Africa. Afterward I had Shauna — Miss McNary, as a private nurse for a while. As a matter of fact she was the one who suggested it might do me good to put everything down on paper. And then, when I showed it to her, she said it was too good just to throw out. She helped me find an agent through another writer patient she'd nursed earlier. I owe her a great deal." His arm tightened around Robyn, pulling her close again. Huskily he added, "Look, I'm really not all that interested in talking about my grandmother's nurse right now."

He slid his other arm around her, molding their bodies together. Robyn had carefully buttoned and tucked her blouse in, but she could feel the warmth of his naked chest through the thin material. She steeled herself to ignore the wild response that threatened to rise and engulf her again.

"Does she know you — *we* are married?"

"I don't know." He hesitated, frowned. "No, I suppose not." His seeking lips nuzzled her throat, nibbled her ear, teased tantalizingly at the corner of her mouth. "Let's go over to the sofa."

Stars danced dizzily inside Robyn's head.

She wanted to go with him, ached to abandon everything in a wild ecstasy of lovemaking. She loved him — he wanted her. This was no act for some onlooker's benefit. He wanted her. She could feel it in every muscle of his body.

But that was just it, she thought despairingly. She *loved* him but he only *wanted* her.

"I'm going upstairs," she said stiffly. "To a room of my own."

He lifted his head. "What is this? A few minutes ago you were as eager as I am." Half angrily he added, "We are legally married."

"Not a real marriage."

His lips twisted. "Don't you have what nice, sensible girls always want? The license, the ceremony, the ring on your finger? And a damned expensive one at that."

Robyn gasped at the implication that she was somehow bought and paid for. She struggled to free herself from his grip that had changed from caressing to cruel.

"I don't understand this," he said harshly. "I know damn well you're not exactly indifferent to me." As if to prove it, he trailed tantalizing fingertips across her lips and she trembled beneath his touch. "Some women have to struggle to respond. Right now I can feel you struggling *not* to respond to me."

It was true. She didn't want to respond to

him. And yet it took every ounce of her strength to hold her body rigid and un-yielding, to resist that overpowering temptation to melt against him.

He grabbed her shoulders and looked darkly into her eyes. "So loosen up," he said roughly. "You want me as much as I want you. We might as well get something for ourselves out of this marriage trap!"

Robyn stared incredulously at him. So he was going to get something out of this "marriage trap" was he! And what would that something be? Herself! Was she a slave to be bound and delivered over to her master's whim?

Furious, she raised her hand and slapped the open palm hard across his cheek.

Chapter Eight

Robyn lay in the unfamiliar bed, uncomfortably wrapped in a bath towel as a makeshift nightgown. She had stormed up the stairs and locked herself in the first bedroom she came to, thinking only belatedly that her belongings were still in Trev's room. She was too proud and angry to go and ask him for them. And he, of course, was too stubborn and arrogant to offer to bring her things to her, she thought furiously. She had heard him pass by her door only minutes after she locked it, his heavy, angry footsteps never pausing.

How dare he try to turn this farce into a *real* wedding night? How dare he ply her with champagne and seductive caresses, no doubt laughing to himself all the time at what an easy conquest she was? And she would have been an easy conquest, she thought, humiliation flaming her face even in the darkness, if that ringing phone and feminine voice hadn't shocked her into coming to her senses. He was cold and calculating, cynically deciding that as long as he was caught in this trap he might as well grab whatever fringe benefits were available.

That was the way he thought of her, Robyn thought, cringing with humiliation, a fringe benefit to be taken for his own physical gratification because she happened to be handy. How could she ever have thought herself in love with such a calculating, arrogant man?

And yet, even as she thought that, she knew despairingly that she was still in love with him. Even now, hurt and angry as she was, her traitorous body ached for his caresses. Even as she despised the way he had deliberately set the scene to seduce her, a part of her wished she had recklessly ignored that ringing phone.

No — no! That was unthinkable madness, she thought shakily. She should never have let the situation go that far, dangerously close to being completely out of control. From now on she would see to it that Trev made the best of this situation on *her* terms, and that meant that whatever affection was displayed was strictly for Mrs. Barrone's benefit. She would have Luther move her clothes first thing in the morning. She was beyond caring what the servants thought now.

There was perhaps one benefit in all this, Robyn thought grimly. Trev had done his worst with his cruel, humiliating words about getting something for himself out of this "marriage trap." He couldn't possibly hurt her any more than he already had.

But, with Shauna McNary's arrival the following day, Robyn began to suspect she was wrong.

Robyn was having lunch in Mrs. Barrone's room when the new nurse arrived. By that time Robyn's things were safely moved to the new room. At the last minute she had weakened and moved everything herself, unwilling to face Luther's carefully guarded curiosity. The new room was smaller but no less luxurious than the master bedroom. Now, Mrs. Barrone had just mischievously admitted that it was she who had had Mrs. Bundy bring the leftover wedding cake to the house and give it to the cook for safe storage in the freezer.

Robyn's first introduction to Shauna McNary was the sound of lilting laughter from down the hallway, a murmur of voices, then more laughter. Robyn's eyes widened when the new nurse stepped into the room, followed by Trev.

She certainly did not fit Robyn's preconceived notion of what a capable, efficient nurse should look like. She had long blond hair, artfully tousled, a honey tan in spite of the winter season, wide-set green eyes, and a lush figure. She was wearing fashionably slim pants and high-heeled boots, dangling earrings and a silky blouse that revealed every inch of well-shaped breasts and slim waist. She was at least nine or ten years older than Robyn, but she managed to make Robyn feel old and dowdy. And this was the nurse Trev had hired because she was so "capable and competent."

Trev made introductions. Shauna had evidently already been informed of the marriage. From the casual, almost indifferent way she appraised Robyn, Robyn wondered angrily if Trev had revealed to her the full circumstances of the marriage.

Later, while Mrs. Barrone was napping, Robyn spied Trev showing Shauna around outside. They were laughing again, an easy companionability that sent a pang through Robyn. Once she saw Shauna touch Trev's arm in a familiar, almost intimate gesture. The three of them had dinner together, Shauna and Trev talking animatedly about mutual acquaintances from San Francisco, Los Angeles and New York. Shauna, it appeared, specialized in wealthy, famous clients. Afterward Trev and Shauna sat on the sofa, with, what seemed to Robyn, unnecessary closeness, looking at snapshots Shauna had brought.

When Robyn went up to bed, they were still sitting in front of the fireplace. Then the reality of the sickening situation hit her. Trev intended to carry on with Shauna under this very roof while Robyn was forced to stand silently by and watch it happen. He knew Robyn was trapped; he knew she wouldn't dare walk out and risk sending Mrs. Barrone to her death. What he intended to have, Robyn thought bitterly, was his own little harem right here in Caverna Bay.

It was a long time before Robyn heard footsteps pass by her door that night. And, strain as she might, she could not tell if there were one pair of feet or two.

After that the days settled into a routine. Trev had business with his agent and publishers, plus setting up his mineral exploration company. Robyn felt quite unnecessary around the house with Shauna to care for Mrs. Barrone and servants to run the house efficiently. She took to spending most of each day at the shop, working on her usual projects or going to the beach. Larry came by occasionally and she yearned to pour out everything to him, but she forced herself to smile brightly and say everything was fine.

Her days, in fact, were really not much different from those before she met Trev. But now she had to go back to the big house at night, back to the torment of being near the man she loved who only scornfully tolerated her. Back to Shauna's knowing eyes and possessive attitude toward Trev.

The weather was miserable. Caverna Bay was always wet in winter, but this year one soaking storm followed another. The ground was water-logged and soggy.

Trev never attempted to touch Robyn again after their wedding night fiasco. Not that Robyn gave him the opportunity, of course. The best that could be said for the situation, Robyn thought grimly, was that Trev and Shauna were at least discreet in their relationship. She was reasonably certain Mrs. Barrone suspected nothing. But it was agony for Robyn to see the intimate, possessive way Shauna monopolized conversations with Trev at mealtimes, touching him on his hand or arm to emphasize a point, making frequent, pointed references to a past that had not included Robyn. Shauna wore a white uniform during daytime hours, but before dinner she invariably changed to something seductively clinging.

Grudgingly Robyn had to admit Shauna

was an excellent nurse. She took meticulous care of Mrs. Barrone, scrutinized her diet, diligently exercised the injured leg and hip, efficiently bathed and dressed her, and encouraged her to care for her hair and make-up.

But in spite of it all, Mrs. Barrone was slipping steadily. Her memory grew more vague, events of forty years ago were often more clear to her than what had happened only yesterday. Arthritic pain clouded her once lively blue eyes. She spent more time watching television, less using the energy it took to read.

Finally Robyn knew she had to talk to Trev about his grandmother. The time might be coming when she must be moved back to the hospital. Usually, after visiting with Mrs. Barrone for a few minutes each morning, Robyn drove directly to her shop, but this morning she waited until Trev was alone in the little room he used as an office and tapped on the door.

"I think we should have a talk about your grandmother," Robyn said, keeping her voice very impersonal and businesslike.

Trev leaned back in his chair. His sleeves were rolled up to his elbows, revealing powerfully muscled forearms. Robyn had to force herself not to dwell on how those arms had once held her. He waved Robyn to a seat.

"She's getting worse, isn't she?" he said reflectively. "I've talked with Shauna about taking her down to the Daydecker Clinic in San Francisco."

Robyn felt a momentary stab of anger that he had discussed this with Shauna but not with her.

"She won't go, of course, unless we literally force her to," he added, sounding exasperated with her stubbornness.

"You've talked with her about it?"

"Yes."

"Would you like me to talk to her and see if I could convince her to go?" Robyn suggested.

Trev raised a dark eyebrow, and Robyn was unhappily reminded of a similar request he had once made to her. If only she had done what he asked, none of this would have happened. Mrs. Barrone would be safe and happy in Palm Springs. And Robyn herself wouldn't know the heartbreak of loving and being married to this man who didn't love her.

"Shauna and I have discussed it. I don't think there's any point mentioning it to my grandmother any further. It only upsets her."

Robyn had that unpleasant left-out feeling that she sometimes had when she and Trev and Shauna were all together and the two of them were laughing at some private joke. She stood up. "Well, since it appears everything is being discussed and decided without me, I won't bother you any more."

"You're not around much," Trev pointed out. His eyes narrowed. "You seem more concerned about that damn shop than about Grandma."

"That isn't true!" Robyn protested indignantly. "It's just that you and Shauna — I mean, I know she's a professional nurse, so her opinion is more valuable than mine, but —"

"So, now that you're here, what is your opinion?" he inquired.

Robyn sat down again. "Well, nothing specific," she said lamely. "It's just that I have the feeling that she feels she reached the big goal she was living for, to see you safely married. And now that that is accomplished she just — well, she isn't all that determined to live."

"What do you suggest?"

"Maybe another goal. Perhaps a trip she'd like to take or something," Robyn said hesitantly.

"I'm afraid, if you ask the doctor, he'll say

that's out of the question. But I can think of another goal that might be meaningful to her."

"What is that?" Robyn asked with interest.

He leaned forward. "We could give her a great-grandchild to look forward to."

Robyn stared at him, shocked and disbelieving. *"Wh-what?"* she faltered.

"I said —"

"I heard what you said! You can't be serious."

His face was unsmiling, eyes intent. "I can assure you, I'm quite serious. In fact, I've been giving it some thought. It would take at least nine months —"

"It usually does!"

He ignored that. "It's the one thing I think she might feel is worth living for. Think about it."

Think about it! Robyn stood up angrily. "No," she said. "I will not think about it. It's out of the question. This deception that involved just the two of us was perhaps justified for your grandmother's sake, but I will not involve an innocent child!"

Robyn stormed out before he could say anything more. She drove to the shop, angry and disturbed, hardly aware of her surroundings. How could Trev even consider such a thing? It was unthinkable. And yet, even as Robyn raged at him in her thoughts, the idea held a certain wickedly tempting appeal that had nothing to do with benefiting Mrs. Barrone. A child would bind them together. As mother of his child, Trev might even love her. . . .

Then she chastised herself soundly for even momentarily considering such a thing. In spite of his serious demeanor, this surely was not something Trev was seriously considering. More likely he was merely amusing himself by shocking her, and he and Shauna would have a good laugh over it.

Mrs. Barrone continued to weaken. Robyn hated to see the decline and yet she couldn't help thinking guiltily, as she had so many times before, that only Mrs. Barrone's death would release her from this painful situation. And then the realization hit her that she would never truly be free again. She would never be free of her love for Trev.

That was something she would just have to learn to live with, she knew. Perhaps, once all this was over and Trev was far away, she could put all this behind her and begin to pick up the shattered pieces of her life. It appeared, from Mrs. Barrone's sinking condition, that Robyn probably would not have much longer to wait. The thought filled her with both sadness and guilty relief.

And then, astonishingly, Mrs. Barrone's condition improved again. The major reason seemed to be a change in medication the doctor ordered. After days of lying listlessly in bed, she started moving around in the wheelchair again, fussing over her plants. Her appetite improved.

Robyn was delighted, and yet somewhere far back in her mind was a sinking feeling of dismay. Her feelings were wildly confused and conflicting. She desperately wished she was not in love with Trev, and yet being in love filled her with a kind of wonder, an awareness of each day that she had never known before. She wanted to be married to him because she loved him, but she didn't want to be married to him because he didn't love her. She didn't want to be anywhere near him and yet away from him she was miserable. She hated the way she still trembled under his smouldering glances and yet it thrilled her that he looked at her that way. Though he mostly ignored her, Robyn could tell he was not totally indifferent to her. Sometimes, in fact, she had the odd feeling he paid attention to Shauna only to annoy her, even sometimes deliberately glancing her way to see if she was watching. And then she had to laugh wryly at herself. Now she really was grasping at straws! Trev couldn't care less what she thought or felt.

More than once Robyn found herself wondering exactly what Trev's feelings toward Shauna were. Was he just amusing himself with her, "making the best of a bad situation" as he had once cold-bloodedly tried to do with Robyn? Or was there something deeper? Was he only waiting to be rid of Robyn so he could wed Shauna? And if that were so, why hadn't he simply married Shauna to begin with?

Robyn thought she knew the answer to that last question. In spite of being an excellent, capable nurse, Shauna was a bit too flamboyant for Mrs. Barrone ever to approve of her as a *wife*. She had, for one thing, been married and divorced. Her former husband was a Hollywood cameraman, and she had any number of amusing, if slightly scandalous stories to tell about movie personalities. Her after-working-hours wardrobe was almost brazenly seductive.

In short, she just did not fit Mrs. Barrone's image of a "nice, sensible young lady," as Trev had obviously been astute enough to realize.

Sometimes Robyn guiltily wondered if *she* was really the nice, sensible girl Mrs. Barrone thought her to be. If she were really so sensible would she have come so close to making love with Trev that night? Would she let herself be aroused almost beyond control by a man she knew didn't love her? A sensible girl would never have let herself fall in love with Trev. And there was another thought that lingered tantalizingly in the back of Robyn's mind, a shocking thought that she was sure would horrify any really nice, sensible girl.

She mused about that tantalizing thought as she worked at her shop, her clever fingers fashioning a pair of agate earrings or a shell bracelet. She thought about it when she accidentally bumped into Trev in the hallway and his hands touched her shoulders, steadying her, leaving an almost searing imprint. She thought about it as she lay alone in her bed at night, wondering what Trev was doing. The thought tantalized her, tempted her, and made her restless with yearning.

Should she — *could* she do it?

If she were certain Trev was in love with Shauna, Robyn knew she could not do it. If she were absolutely certain he had an intimate physical relationship with Shauna, even without undying love, she didn't think she could do it either.

And yet there was just enough doubt in Robyn's mind about the real relationship between Trev and Shauna to keep her thinking her own shocking thought. She had the feeling there was an intimate relationship between them. Shauna, with her intimate glances and familiar touches, certainly gave that impression. And yet if there were anything going on, they were certainly discreet about it. Once, though ashamed of herself, Robyn had peeked out when she heard footsteps passing her room late at night. It was Trev going to his room. Alone. Of course he could have just come from Shauna's room, but with a book in his hand, Robyn somehow doubted it. Another time Robyn had come home at midafternoon from the gift shop, half expecting to catch Trev and Shauna in some afternoon dalliance while Mrs. Barrone napped. But Trev was working in his office and Shauna closeted alone in her own room.

Robyn decided and changed her mind half a dozen times. What she was considering was insane, totally unthinkable! And yet another part of her recklessly retorted, so what? She and Trev were legally married. Why not do as Trev had suggested and grab something for herself out of this "marriage trap"? Mrs. Barrone had lived far beyond any reasonable expectation and, from all appearances, might live a lot longer. Still Robyn knew she couldn't do it as coldbloodedly as Trev suggested, couldn't do it except for one all-compelling reason. She loved him. If this were all she could ever have of him, why not take it? Why not grab what he offered before she was left with only regrets and empty arms?

And yet, there just didn't seem to be any suitable opportunity. She couldn't just brazenly march into his room and throw herself at him! The time and place had to be right. Not that she was afraid she had hurt his feelings or damaged his ego that night. He was too arrogantly self-assured for that. But she had made her "no" emphatic.

But the opportunity simply was not there. In the evening Mrs. Barrone expected either Robyn or Trev, or both of them, to spend some time with her. Any other time in the evenings that Trev and Robyn might have had alone, Shauna was invariably present. Almost as if she were a chaperone, Robyn thought in frustration, a chaperone who definitely had designs on the man herself.

Then, suddenly, the opportunity arose. Aid came from an unexpected source. The Internal Revenue Service was auditing Shauna's tax returns for a couple of years back and she had to go down to San Francisco for a meeting with them. She left on a Tuesday, expecting to return sometime between Thursday and Friday evenings.

Mrs. Barrone had to have some injections,

which Robyn could not give, so Trev hired Mrs. Bundy to come back for a few days.

The first night Shauna was gone Trev disappeared into his office immediately after dinner and stayed there. Robyn wondered if he was deliberately avoiding her.

The following night Trev invited Dr. Helgeson to dinner. Mrs. Barrone was feeling well enough to have her dinner with them, the first time she had done so. Marie made a Beef Wellington and Dr. Helgeson brought a bottle of red wine. It was a marvelous evening with much laughter and congenial conversation. What made it even more pleasant for Robyn was that Shauna was not there to act as if she, not Robyn, were the one married to Trev.

Mrs. Bundy tucked Mrs. Barrone into bed not too long after dinner, but Dr. Helgeson stayed fairly late. Afterward Robyn peeked in on Mrs. Barrone and heard the slow, steady sounds of her breathing. There was still a lamp on in the living room and she walked over to turn it out before going up the stairs to bed.

She had just snapped the switch off when she realized Trev hadn't already gone up to bed as she had thought. He was stretched out on the floor in front of the fireplace, a glass of wine on the hearth beside him.

"That's much better with the light off," he said approvingly. "There's a bit of wine left. Would you like a glass?"

Robyn caught her breath, suddenly aware of the dim, romantic firelight, the setting that was almost identical to their wedding night. She should turn and run, she thought wildly, run for her life. She couldn't go through with this, *mustn't* go through with it!

He turned to look up at her lazily. "Well?" he murmured. Was his voice mocking — or challenging? There was something in its husky murmur that set her heart pounding.

"Yes, thank you. I'd like a glass," she said primly.

She sat on the sofa, one leg tucked under her, while he went to a cabinet under the balcony and brought another glass. He drained the liquid, glowing red-gold in the firelight, into the glass and handed it to her. She expected him to sit down beside her and tensed herself for the giddy weakness that his nearness always aroused in her, but he went back to sit on the floor in front of the fire.

"I think Grandma enjoyed coming to the dining room for dinner," he remarked casually.

"Yes," Robyn agreed. "Though it might be

too much for her on a regular basis."

"Probably."

He lapsed into silence. The firelight highlighting his dark hair turned his eyes into shadowed hollows, his skin to bronze. Motionless, broodingly, he stared into the dying coals. "Gift shop getting along all right?" he asked finally.

Robyn jumped, startled by the unexpectedly prosaic question. Her own mind certainly had not been on the gift shop, she thought shakily, glad the dim light hid her flush of embarrassment. The fragile stem of the wine glass felt slippery under her damp hands.

"It's fine, thank you. A chartered bus stopped last weekend and I made quite a few sales."

"Your friend Larry still around?"

Robyn hesitated, wondering uneasily why he should ask that. "He stopped by and left an order for another dozen of my mobiles."

More silence. Robyn watched him from under discreetly half-lowered lids, puzzled. He seemed to be ignoring her, and yet some unseen vibration between them told her instinctively that his elaborate display of indifference was not real. But why the pretense? He had jumped at the opportunity to make love to her on their wedding night.

But he was certainly making no jumps now. He started another idle conversation, something about a bad storm that was predicted to blow in within the next few days. As if to collaborate his words rain spattered against the big west windows and a gust of wind shrieked around the fireplace. She searched her mind for some way to subtly let him know that her feelings had changed since their wedding night fiasco.

He stretched out prone on the floor again. Robyn's mouth went dry as she thought of that other night, his naked chest pressed against her own thundering heart, the feeling of his hands roaming unrestrainedly over her, her own shuddering reaction. . . .

He rolled over to face her, head supported on one hand. "Penny for your thoughts."

He had said that the other night too. Robyn licked dry lips, suddenly embarrassed by what she had been thinking. But he couldn't read her mind, she thought shakily. He couldn't know what wild, not at all "nice, sensible girl" thoughts whirled through her mind.

"Nothing," she said barely above a whisper. She cleared her throat and a bit more loudly said, "I was just enjoying the fire and — and not thinking anything at all."

"Weren't you?" The words were a mocking

blend of accusation and challenge.

Robyn took a gulp of wine to hide the blaze of color that she was afraid might be visible on her face even in the dim light. He couldn't know what she was thinking. He couldn't! And yet she had no doubt that he did know. His face, turned away from the fire, was all in shadows now. His lean figure was only a dark relaxed silhouette on the floor. And yet relaxed with the readiness of a predator ever poised to strike.

One part of her wanted to run but another part recklessly demanded that she stay. Yes, yes — why not? she thought wildly. She wanted this, wanted it as much as he did. She loved him. Even if he only *wanted* her, she loved him.

She tensed, waiting for the touch of his hand that would melt her like a snowflake caught in the flame. But he didn't touch her.

"You haven't answered my question," he said softly.

Robyn stared at him, painfully aware of her own ragged breathing. He wasn't going to make any move toward her. He wanted her. She knew that. But this time she was going to have to come to him. He wasn't going to make it easy for her.

She couldn't do it! She couldn't just — just brazenly seduce a man! Why was he humiliating her like this? She had made herself available, why didn't he take the initiative now?

He wasn't going to do it. And neither could she, she thought helplessly. It just wasn't in her. She stood up on rubbery legs that she hoped would somehow carry her up the stairs.

Unbelievingly, she felt her legs buckle beneath her, not in a fall, but as if some almost magnetic force were pulling her to the lush carpet. Trev rolled to a sitting position.

"Did you hurt yourself?"

"No, I — I just —" The words thickened around Robyn's dry tongue. Then with a boldness she found almost unrecognizable in herself she added, "I just thought — I mean, you've had a hard day. Would you like me to rub your back?"

Silence. Surprise? Scorn? It was the tactic he had used, she thought defiantly. Why shouldn't she use it too?

Then slowly, ever so slowly, he started unbuttoning his shirt. He stripped it off, a bronzed god in the firelight. Robyn watched, mesmerized. Slowly he moved around to turn his back to her. She had to wipe the damp perspiration from her hands before she could reach up and rub her hands over that smoothly muscled back.

She massaged the sinewy cords along his neck and shoulders, lightly kneaded the long muscles along either side of his spine. Then softly, hardly believing her own daring, she touched her lips lightly to the back of his neck.

She felt his body go rigid, but he didn't turn to face her. His voice was strangely muffled when he spoke.

"Why did you do that? Why are you acting like this?"

Why? she thought wildly. *Because I love you. Because it's all I can ever have of you and I'm desperate enough to settle for anything.*

But she couldn't say that, of course. What she was doing was bad enough without adding the agony of admitting she loved a man who did not love her.

"Because I've decided you were right," she said. "We might as well get something for ourselves out of this marriage we're trapped in. We might as well make the best of the situation and — grab the fringe benefits."

He swiveled around slowly to face her. She thought he was going to take her in his arms. A chunk of log flickered into flames and she saw the expression on his face. There was no mistaking the disgust and contempt.

"I — I mean —" she faltered.

"I know what you mean," he said harshly. He snatched up the discarded shirt and stalked across the carpeted floor and stairs. A moment later the slam of his bedroom door reverberated through the house.

Robyn stared after him, too astonished for a moment to move, then suddenly sickened. She had thrown herself at him and he had turned her down cold. He didn't want her. Shock and humiliation flooded over her like ice water.

Was it because of Shauna? Was he in love with her? Or was it simply that his dislike and distaste for Robyn was so strong that he didn't want her even on a purely sexual basis? That look of utter, scathing contempt burned in her mind, her soul.

What did it matter why he had rejected her? He had done it. The humiliation was a physical pain, a throbbing ache that engulfed her. She had offered herself to him and he had walked away.

She couldn't stay here any longer, she thought, dazed as she somehow staggered up the stairs. It was impossible now. She must go. Mrs. Barrone was stronger now. They could tell her something. But Robyn knew she couldn't hang on any longer.

Chapter Nine

Robyn carefully avoided Trev the following day. She deliberately went down late in the morning so she wouldn't have to breakfast with him, then hurried over to spend the day at her shop. In the clear light of day her thought that they could tell Mrs. Barrone "something" didn't sound so simple. It was true that Mrs. Barrone seemed to be improving. But what would the shock of an abrupt split between Trev and Robyn do to her? It was the same old problem. Nothing was changed. And yet Robyn knew she couldn't go on like this much longer. She couldn't, not after the humiliation of Trev's rejection, the look of disbelieving scorn on his face.

As it turned out, the matter was out of Robyn's hands.

Shauna returned Thursday evening, smug over having somehow won her argument with the Internal Revenue Service. Shauna always wins, Robyn thought, listening to her vivacious account of the meeting with the IRS. Robyn excused herself and went to visit with Mrs. Barrone when Shauna launched into a flurry of gossip she had also picked up on the trip about people she and Trev knew. Robyn doubted that her presence would be missed.

And then, sometime during the night, Mrs. Barrone quite peacefully died. Trev called an ambulance and they rushed her to the hospital again, but it was too late. The doctor said it was another, and this time far more devastating, stroke.

Robyn was at first flooded with a terrible sense of guilt, wondering if her thoughts of leaving had somehow communicated themselves to Mrs. Barrone and caused the stroke. But then, after the first shock had worn off and she could think more calmly, she was able to discard that illogical thought. She searched her mind and was positive she had revealed nothing of her inner turmoil. Mrs. Barrone had died happy, secure in the belief that her grandson was happily wed to Robyn. But that comforting knowledge couldn't keep the tears of regret for the loss of an old and dear friend from falling from Robyn's eyes.

Trev grimly and silently went about making the necessary arrangements. The predicted storm had not yet arrived, but the weather was cold and drizzly. Robyn was tempted to move out immediately now that the need for this marriage charade was over, but as a final gesture of respect to Mrs. Barrone she decided to stay on until after the funeral. What she did was of little importance anyway, she thought. No one seemed to notice her.

She packed her things and quietly carried everything down to her car when no one was watching. She tried several times to contact Larry, but he was evidently off on one of his frequent trips.

The funeral was held Monday afternoon at the same little church where Trev and Robyn had been married. That morning the overdue storm hit the coast with unleashed fury. Torrents of rain fell and wind whipped the bay into towering waves. Water streamed across the streets and electric lines flapped in the wind.

In spite of the storm, most of the town turned out for the funeral. Trev, Robyn, Shauna and Dr. Helgeson sat together in a front pew. Tears slipped quietly from Robyn's downcast eyes as the minister and then two old friends of Mrs. Barrone's spoke. Robyn was surprised and touched that Trev had arranged for that additional little gesture; Mrs. Barrone would have liked it.

It was painful standing so close to Trev,

feeling the touch of his shoulder against hers. She reminded herself that she was free now, no longer trapped. But she knew that even after that cruel, humiliating rejection she would never be free of her love for Trev. It was a part of her now — now and forever. Her only consolation was a certain grim satisfaction in the knowledge that she had never revealed that love to him.

An explosive blast of wind hit the little church. The floor shuddered beneath uneasy feet. Even the minister momentarily paused in his speaking. Usually Robyn felt a certain wild exhilaration in a storm, but there was no such feeling now. She felt empty, drained.

When they returned, the big house seemed silent and desolate. Robyn wondered how she was going to get out without anyone seeing her. She wanted to avoid any sort of questions or explanations or good-byes, and most especially the look of smug victory on Shauna's lovely face.

She went up to her room and changed from the dark dress she had worn to the funeral to the one outfit she had left unpacked, a comfortable knit pantsuit. She peered carefully out the door, retreating when she saw Trev and Shauna in the living room below. She paced the room restlessly, stared with unseeing eyes at the wildly waving treetops on the ridge above the house.

What was she going to do now? Move back to the apartment behind the gift shop, she supposed, take up life where it was before this strange interlude. Maybe she'd even marry Larry someday, she thought vaguely. Perhaps an easygoing, friendly relationship was preferable to the agony of love.

But suddenly Robyn knew she didn't want to go back to the apartment right now. Not yet. Trev would be around Caverna Bay for a little while yet, until he could finish things up here and put the house on the market. Trev and *Shauna* would be around, she thought grimly. No, she couldn't face that, looking across the bay from her little bedroom each night, seeing the lights of the big house, knowing Trev and Shauna were here together with no longer any need to be discreet.

She would go away somewhere until they were gone, she decided. She started toward the door again. Suddenly she remembered something else. The rings. They were so familiar on her hand now that she had almost forgotten them. She found herself strangely reluctant to remove them, as if doing so were breaking some last bond between herself and Trev. But that was ridiculous, she reminded herself. There never had been any real bonds between them, only the trap that had somehow closed around them. She jerked the rings off and left them in plain sight on the dressing table. She surely wasn't about to run off with the precious diamonds Trev had bought as an "investment."

She opened the door and carefully peeked out again. She saw no one in the living room below now. She listened a moment but heard no one moving around. She picked up her purse and the sack containing her dress, draping her jacket over the cosmetics case to conceal it should she accidentally run into one of the servants.

She slipped quietly down the stairs. A figure stepped out from under the concealing balcony. Trevor! He was still wearing the dark suit he had worn to the funeral.

His eyes flicked over her change of clothing and the jacket she carried. "Going somewhere?"

"I — I wanted to take care of a few things over at the shop." Her voice quivered. She was not a good liar in spite of the long, involved deception played on Mrs. Barrone.

"There are some things we have to talk about," he said.

Robyn lifted her head. "I'm sure the prenuptial agreement your lawyer drew up takes care of everything," she replied aloofly.

"Damn the prenuptial agreement!" he exploded. "I want to know —"

Robyn felt suddenly dizzy. She couldn't handle all this now, the messy details of the divorce, the tying up of any loose threads of their relationship. "Please," she said faintly. "I — I just don't feel up to talking now."

He hesitated a moment, then stepped back. "Of course. I'm sorry. I suppose it isn't the best time." He hesitated again, brow furrowing. "But couldn't these matters at the shop wait until later? The storm —"

"I'm sure it has about blown itself out," Robyn said. She hurried on by him, relieved that he had evidently accepted her story.

In the spacious three-car garage she tossed her cosmetics case and sack into the already crowded back seat of her car. She pressed the button controlling the electrically operated garage doors, hesitating a moment as a sheet of wind-driven rain slanted through the open doors. Her remark that the storm had about blown itself out was hardly accurate. If anything, the wind and rain had increased in fury. The smaller trees and shrubs around the house tossed crazily in the shrieking wind. Above the wind she could hear the redwoods creaking and groaning as if protesting this attack of nature on a rampage. A running sheet of water covered the driveway. Robyn hesitated, wondering if it was unwise to venture out in this.

She glanced back at the door leading to the interior part of the house. No, she decided, she wasn't going back. She would take her chances with the storm rather than stay another night under the same roof with Trev and Shauna.

She backed the car out of the garage, feeling it shudder around her as the wind buffeted it. She inched her way down the sloping, water-sheeted driveway. Her busy windshield wipers could barely keep up with the pounding rain. Darkness had not yet fallen but the car headlights barely penetrated the grayness of clouds and rain. The distance to the iron gates seemed interminable as she crept along.

She kept reminding herself she was free now. But somehow, instead of feeling happy or even relieved, she only felt regret. Regret that she had not gone through that wedding night with Trev. At least she would have had that to remember, a memory no one could take from her. Now she hadn't even a memory.

Suddenly something interrupted her disjointed thoughts. A sound, a straining vibration — she braked uncertainly, trying to peer through the curtains of rain. She was deep into the corridor of redwoods, the mighty trunks looking almost unreal around her, a forest of prehistoric giants, their heads lost in the storm. Maybe she should turn around and go back —

An ominous rumble, a shuddering groan — and then the earth seemed to move beneath Robyn. The little car rattled and shook. The roar crashed in Robyn's ears, vibrated through her body, caught her like a terrier shaking a rat. She clutched the steering wheel, eyes wide with fear and shock. What was happening?

The vibrations died away like retreating thunder. After that incredible earth-shattering crash, wind and rain seemed almost inconsequential. Robyn apprehensively turned around in the seat, but the rain-flooded rear window was impossible to see through. Cautiously she opened the side window and peered outside. She still couldn't see anything, but the usual scent of the redwoods was strangely intensified. Uncertainly she peered ahead again, afraid to go on without knowing the source of that tremendous crash.

Then she saw what it was. She slipped out of the car and stood there, unconscious of the rain pouring down on her bare head. A redwood had fallen. One of those giants of the forest, its shallow roots water-soaked by the extraordinarily wet weather, had come crashing down under the force of the wind. It had fallen directly across the driveway behind her; its size seemed even more incredible now that it lay on the ground.

Robyn fought off hysteria. She realized death had missed her by little more than inches. Only a few seconds delay and her little car would have been directly in the path of that crashing giant.

Over the shrieking wind she heard something else — a voice? It galvanized her into action. Someone was evidently already coming from the house to investigate that terrible crash, and she must get away before they arrived.

She put the car in gear, trying not to think that another of the giant redwoods might come thundering down at any moment. At the iron gates she realized she had been holding her breath, and she released it shakily. Here the trees were more protected from the wind and the danger was lessened.

She glanced back apprehensively and then realized suddenly that there was no particular need to hurry away from the big house now. No one else was going to be leaving there for a while, not with the road blocked by that redwood. Trev and Shauna were trapped there until the road could be cleared. Not that that situation was apt to bother them, she thought bitterly. They might even find it enjoyable, now that there was no longer any need for them to sneak around to be together.

At the junction of South Bay Road and the main highway, Robyn hesitated again. The most sensible thing to do would be to go directly to her little apartment behind the shop. But it was possible that when she didn't return to the big house, Trev would call her. She couldn't talk to him. She needed time to get her emotions sorted out.

Resolutely she turned south, away from Caverna Bay. She intended to put as much distance as possible between herself and the big house where Trev and Shauna were doubtless snugly entrapped. Turning on the radio, she found that the storm was buffeting the coast all the way to San Francisco. She decided to stop early at a motel. She was also uncomfortably wet from the time she had spent standing in the rain staring at the fallen tree.

In the morning she drove on south, still with no definite idea as to where she was heading. The storm had passed through, leaving reports of minor roads flooded, trees down, and power outages all along the coast. Leaves, broken limbs and rivulets of running water were everywhere. At San Francisco she turned inland, somehow knowing that even as much as she loved the sea she didn't want to be near it now. She knew she couldn't look at it without seeing Trev as she had seen him that first time, standing with his back to it: harsh, powerful, primitively masculine.

She drove all the way across the state and into Arizona, finally reaching Phoenix. The weather was warm and dry, the desert landscape totally different from Caverna Bay. She stayed at a motel east of the city, swam in the pool and hiked in the nearby Superstition Mountains. They were dry and barren mountains, nothing like the tree covered slopes back home. She met a pleasant young lawyer vacationing in Arizona from his home back east. She ate her fill of spicy, authentic Mexican food.

There was nothing at all to remind her of Trev. It was a place as different from Caverna Bay as she could hope to find. A whole new world. Exactly what she had wanted to find.

And yet Trev was never out of her mind. Everything reminded her of him. A dark-haired man seen across a room, a car that looked like his, a laugh that for a moment sounded like his, would set her heart racing. She fought a constant battle with depression and tears. Even as she laughed or swam with the young lawyer, her thoughts always circled back to Trev. Had he filed for divorce yet? Perhaps he would go to Nevada for a hurried decree, so he would be free to marry Shauna as soon as possible.

Robyn had left Caverna Bay to avoid seeing Trev again, and yet the thought that he might still be there was strangely tantalizing. How deeply she suddenly ached to see him. It was humiliating, she thought, as she remembered again how he had reacted to her advances that night.

She had planned to stay away a full three weeks, thinking that would surely give Trev plenty of time to leave and erase forever any chance of seeing him again. But at the end of two weeks, she packed up and started home. She told herself it was because of finances. She had run out of money quickly because she hadn't brought much cash and she was almost afraid to consider the bills she had run up on her credit cards. But she knew that wasn't the real reason she was suddenly almost desperately eager to return to Caverna Bay.

She arrived after dark on a midweek evening. Rain had fallen earlier but now only a few dark clouds scudded across the sky and stars glimmered between them. It seemed as if she had been gone a long, long time. She was almost surprised to see that the town was the same. Even the faded "Welcome to Caverna Bay" sign still flapped over Main Street.

Deliberately she forced herself not to look back at the south side of the bay. Her feelings were more conflicting and confusing than ever. Afraid Trev might still be here. Afraid Shauna might be with him. Afraid he might not be here.

The shop looked lonely and a bit forlorn as she stopped the car in the narrow driveway. She unlocked the apartment door and carried a few things inside, deciding wearily that she would leave the rest until morning. She hadn't been home more than half an hour when a knock sounded at the door. Her heart flip-flopped. Had Trev been watching from the big house window and seen her arrive?

She hurried to the door, struggling to compose herself.

"Larry!" she gasped, unable to keep the disappointment from her voice. Hurriedly she added more welcomingly, "Come on in."

"I just saw the lights and wondered —" Larry peered around uneasily. "You're alone?"

Robyn closed the door, surprised. She had assumed word of her defection would be all over town by now. But she had evidently attached too much importance to herself, she thought wryly. Trev obviously hadn't thought her leaving important enough to mention to anyone.

"I'm alone," she said noncommittally.

"What the hell is going on anyway?" he demanded. "I was out of town and by the time I got back Mrs. Barrone was dead and buried. Then I heard something about some big fuss at Barrone's house the night of the funeral. Now the gates to the place are closed and padlocked."

Yes, Robyn thought wryly, there had undoubtedly been a "big fuss" when Trev and Shauna tore themselves away from each other long enough to discover that giant redwood blocking the driveway. The thought of Trev standing at the window hopefully watching for her return now seemed pathetically ridiculous.

"No one is living there then?" she asked dully.

"Doesn't appear to be. I drove up there. I was worried about you."

Robyn turned away and busied herself adjusting the thermostat to hide the tears springing to her eyes. He was gone then. There was no longer any doubt about it, no longer any hope that her wild dreams about him might somehow come true. He was gone, gone forever, and the hopeless, numbing truth hit her with the force of the falling redwood.

Chapter Ten

Robyn gave Larry a rather edited version of the breakup between herself and Trev, more or less trying to shrug it off as just one of those things that didn't work out. Larry diplomatically refrained from saying, "I told you so."

He hung around Caverna Bay, working on his paintings for the busy summer season, postponing his usual trips out of town. He was helpful, unaccusing, sensitively attuned to her moods. Robyn unhappily wished she had fallen in love with him before she met Trev. She almost desperately wished she could fall in love with him now. But she couldn't. He was, and always would be, simply a very dear friend. In spite of her earlier thoughts that a quiet companionship might be preferable to the agonies of love, she knew she could never marry him on that basis. She tried to tell him as much, but he just shushed her and told her there was plenty of time. But Robyn unhappily knew that while time might dull the ache of her pain, it would never erase her love for Trev.

No one seemed to know exactly what had happened at the big house across the bay. Robyn, out of curiosity, drove up to the locked iron gates one day. Impulsively she climbed through the fence and walked up the driveway. She didn't approach the house. It had a deserted, unused appearance even from a distance. The redwood tree had been cut into several sections and heavy equipment evidently used to drag the huge pieces out of the road.

Beth Hylder stopped in a few days later and mentioned that her logger husband was the one who had been hired to clear the driveway with his equipment. It had been done a week or so after the funeral. Her husband hadn't seen anyone in the big house except the servants.

So what had been the "big fuss" the night she left? Robyn wondered, puzzled. She asked a few questions around town, but no one seemed certain. A lot of lights, someone said. Maybe a siren. So much had gone on in that storm; a carload of people had careened down a mountain road, a man had suffered a heart attack while trying to nail down his roof — the goings-on at the big house had been incidental.

Larry knew she was always thinking about Trev. She had confessed as much. He was patient and understanding for the first two or three weeks, then impatient, and finally angry. Robyn never defended herself. She found her hopeless love for Trev almost indefensible. But it was there.

She kept thinking she would hear from Trev's lawyer or be served with divorce papers, but nothing happened. She thought only briefly of filing for the divorce herself, then stubbornly decided that Trev had married her, he would have to divorce her. The only question was, why wasn't he doing it? It was possible, she supposed, that if he had gone out of the state or country to get the divorce that she wouldn't be notified. She felt as though she were drifting in limbo. She found she missed her former visits with Mrs. Barrone too, missed her cheerful, sometimes tart remarks. She tried to live from day to day, frightened by the bleak, lonely future that faced her.

Then one Saturday afternoon Larry walked into the shop with an odd expression on his face. He tossed a folded piece of paper on the counter. "It's Trev's address." Larry hesitated. "Or at least where he was a few weeks ago."

The unexpected information hit Robyn like a shock wave. A dozen questions ricocheted through her mind. What was he doing? Was Shauna with him? What about the divorce? In a strangled voice she finally managed to ask, "Where — where did you get this?"

"I sweet-talked it out of a pretty little nurse over at Redwood Valley Hospital. My charms work on *some* women," he added in a wry tone.

Robyn didn't notice the small jibe. "Hospital!" she gasped. "But what's wrong? What happened?"

Larry explained that he had done a little private sleuthing about what had happened at the big house after Robyn's departure. He learned that an out-of-town ambulance had gone up there that night and had taken Trev to the Redwood Valley Hospital. A short time later he had been flown down to a clinic in San Francisco at the address on the paper. "Of course, there's no telling if he's still there or not. It's been quite a while," Larry finished.

Six weeks and one day since she fled the house across the bay, Robyn knew without calculating. "But what could have happened to him?" she questioned. "Was he sick or hurt or —"

"An accident of some kind. The girl I talked to thought he was pretty badly off, but she didn't know exactly what was wrong. She got me the address of this clinic where he was taken. Daydecker, or something like that."

The Daydecker Clinic, Robyn thought, dazed. Yes, that was where Trev had wanted to take his grandmother. And then a horrifying thought hit her. After all this time, anything could have happened. He could be dead by now! She clutched the counter for support as her knees threatened to give way beneath her. Dear God, no — he couldn't be dead.

Larry looked alarmed. "Robyn, what's wrong? I thought you'd want to know where he was."

"I — I did — I do — want to know. Oh, Larry, thank you. I'm sorry. It was just for a moment there I thought of something."

"That he might be dead?"

Robyn nodded wordlessly.

"I guess if I ever had any doubts about how much you love him, I don't have any now. That look on your face says it all." He patted her shoulder sympathetically. "I hope he's okay. I really do."

"Thank you, Larry. Why did you do all this?"

He gave her a crooked grin. "I kept thinking that with him gone you'd turn to me. I finally got it through my head that it wasn't going to happen. For a while I was angry.

But I still care enough about you to want you to be happy. I just hope it helps."

Larry left and Robyn sat on her stool by the counter, one hand on the telephone, afraid to dial, afraid of what she might find out. She was still puzzled by what sort of accident could have happened at the big house that night. She didn't want to know — and yet she had to know. Shakily she picked up the phone to dial the long distance number.

"Daydecker Clinic."

"Could you tell me if you have — or did have a patient by the name of Trevor Barrone?" Robyn had to struggle to force her voice above a frightened whisper.

The answer was prompt, businesslike. "Yes, he's in room three-twenty-eight. Would you like me to connect you?"

Relief collided with panic. He was alive — alive! But she couldn't talk to him yet. She wasn't prepared. She had to think, to collect herself. "No, I — I'll come in to see him," she said.

She hung up quickly, her hands trembling. He was alive! And yet, if he were still in the hospital after all this time, something must be seriously wrong. She had to find out.

She was on her way early the following morning. It had all happened so quickly that she felt dazed. But now that she was on her way, she wondered how he would feel about seeing her. Why hadn't he let her know what had happened? Was Shauna with him?

She arrived at the Clinic at midafternoon. It was a spring day. The parking lot was crowded with Sunday afternoon visitors. She walked inside and got a visitor's card from the receptionist. She took the elevator to the third floor and followed the arrows down a hall and around a corner.

The door was open. It was a private room. He was lying in the hospital bed, idly leafing through a magazine, a familiar half-scowl on his face.

Robyn's heart flip-flopped erratically. She wanted to run and throw herself on him and yet her legs felt frozen. He looked almost achingly familiar — lean, angular face, with the thin scar along the jawline, lock of dark hair falling negligently across his forehead, well-shaped hands restlessly turning pages. He looked pale, all traces of tan gone now. His eyes were deeply shadowed.

Suddenly he looked up, his glance catching her poised there in the doorway. His look of shocked surprise was quickly replaced by a carefully guarded expression.

"Why didn't you tell me?" Robyn asked. "Why didn't you let me know?"

"Obviously because I didn't want you to know," he said. His eyes narrowed. "How did you find out?"

"Larry did a little private detective work."

"Of course. Good old Larry."

Robyn took a few steps toward the bed, but his unwelcoming gaze stopped her. "But I don't understand. What happened?"

"I thought there was something a little odd about the way you rushed out to take care of something at the shop immediately after the funeral. I went up to your room and found your wedding rings on the dressing table. I knew then you weren't planning to come back. I went after you but you had already started down the driveway. I ran after you, thinking I could catch up with you and stop you."

He paused, as if the effort of the explanation had tired him. Robyn watched him with growing horror. The scar stood out like a ragged white line on his tensed jaw.

He went on, his voice curiously flat and expressionless. "The storm blew a redwood down. One of the branches caught me when it fell. It injured my back." He laughed, a harsh, humorless sound. "That's ironic, isn't it? I made it through a couple of hundred miles of jungle hell only to be felled by a tree in my own backyard."

That voice she had heard! It wasn't just someone coming from the house to investigate the crash. It was Trev, trapped and injured under the tree. And she had driven away and left him lying there helpless!

"I suppose I shouldn't complain though," Trev added grimly. "A few more feet and I'd have been directly under the tree and wouldn't be alive to tell about it."

"I'm sorry," she whispered, white-faced, shaken by remorse. "I didn't know."

He shrugged. "It was fortunate for me that Shauna was still at the house. As I'm sure you're aware, she is an excellent nurse. She took care of me until the ambulance arrived. The road was blocked, of course, so they had to use a stretcher to carry me around the tree."

Shauna! In her agitation Robyn had forgotten about the attractive nurse. Now she looked around surreptitiously, wondering if Shauna was here caring for Trev. No wonder he preferred Shauna, Robyn thought unhappily. Shauna was there to help him, while Robyn herself had walked away when he needed help. The awful guilt of what she had done made her feel weak and dazed, and she clutched the foot of the bed for support.

"It wasn't fair of you not to tell me what had happened," she said, still unable to get her voice above a whisper. "I had a right to know."

"Why?" he asked harshly. "So you could rush down here and take care of me? Isn't that what you always do, whether it's your own sick aunt or somebody else's grandmother or just a stray seagull? You're always trapped by your own softheartedness. And I won't have a wife on those terms!"

Robyn lifted anguished eyes to his. "On what — what terms will you have a wife?" she asked tremulously, recklessly knowing that she didn't care what the terms were, she'd take them.

But he didn't answer. He just stared into space out the window at the patch of blue sky marked by a spreading jet trail. Robyn glanced around the room, absentmindedly noting the pleasant, beige walls, the television and the neat bedside stand. There were no flowers, nothing to personalize the room except a blue silk robe hanging on a stand by the bed.

"Have you disposed of the house yet?" Robyn asked finally.

"No," he answered briefly. "I told Luther and Marie they might as well close the house up while I was in here. I haven't decided what to do with it yet."

"Is Shauna here?" Robyn asked tentatively, glancing around uneasily again.

"No."

The brusque statement didn't completely answer her question.

"Do you mean she just isn't here at the hospital right now?" she asked uncertainly. "Or —"

"I believe she has taken a job nursing some wealthy rancher over in Arizona. There was no more need for her services, of course, after my grandmother died." His voice was coldly superior and he continued to look out the window.

"I was under the impression that Shauna's talents were not limited solely to her nursing abilities," Robyn retorted.

Trev's head snapped around to face her. "Are you implying there was something going on between Shauna and me while she was taking care of my grandmother?"

"I'm not blind. I could see what was going on!"

"Could you now," he said sarcastically. "And just exactly what did you see?"

Robyn hesitated. "You were always talking to her. Paying attention to her. And she always acted as if she owned you!"

"That's true," he said grimly. "And if there's one thing that turns me off it is a possessive, grabby woman who assumes a lot of things that aren't true."

Robyn hesitated, uncertain if he was referring to Shauna or herself. "Wh— what do you mean?" she faltered.

He straightened in the bed, roughly rearranging the pillow behind his shoulders. "I mean I hired Shauna for the sole reason that she is an extremely capable nurse and I wanted the best for my grandmother. But Shauna thought I had other motives. I had a hard time convincing her otherwise. But there was never, at any time, anything between us while she was there at the house." He hesitated, finally adding slowly, "I'm not saying there wasn't once, but it was for a very short while and it was over a long time ago."

"You could hardly blame Shauna if she thought otherwise," Robyn commented tartly. "You certainly had me fooled."

Trev scowled, rolled the magazine into a tight roll, then straightened and rolled it again. "I suppose she had reason to think what she did," he admitted grudgingly. "I was trying to make you jealous."

Robyn's eyes widened in astonishment.

"It was a cheap trick, I admit it, but you were so damned aloof and untouchable," Trev said.

"And you enjoyed making me miserable

letting me think you were making love to another woman under my nose." Robyn walked around the bed to stand angrily by the window.

"If you were miserable about anything you thought Shauna and I were doing, you certainly hid it well," he snapped. "And I don't think you have any right to act so holier-than-thou. Weren't you carrying on with your 'friend' Larry behind my back?"

"I most certainly was not!" Robyn stormed, infuriated by the unwarranted accusation. "How dare you make such accusations? If it weren't for Larry, I wouldn't even be here now!"

"You shouldn't have come," Trev said dully. He paused when a nurse started to enter the room carrying a tray of medications, checked the room number, and went across the hallway instead. "I don't want any woman feeling sorry for me and thinking she has to stay with me and take care of me because I'm flat on my back and helpless."

Robyn caught her breath. Here they were, arguing and accusing and fighting, and she still didn't know what was wrong with him, how seriously he was injured. "Are you — helpless?" she faltered.

"What does it look like? You don't see me hiking around on the beach, do you? Or chasing the nurses, which is what you no doubt assume I'd be doing if I could."

She ignored the sarcasm, her eyes traveling slowly over his lean figure concealed by the hospital bedsheets. Was he crippled, unable to walk? Her eyes lifted to meet his. "It doesn't matter," she said simply. "I love you."

He regarded her coldly. "See? You're doing it again. You don't love me. You just feel sorry for me. That was why I never wanted you to know I was here. I won't have a wife who says she loves me just because she feels sorry for me!"

"That isn't it —"

"Would you have come rushing down here if I were on my feet and healthy?" He answered the question himself without waiting for her reply. "No, you wouldn't have. You only came for the same reason you were trying to rescue that damn seagull the first time I ever saw you. Because that's the kind of person you are."

Robyn felt dazed and helpless. She stared with unseeing eyes at the city spread out below the hospital window, the bridge across the bay, the streams of traffic. In a way, he was right, she thought slowly. She probably wouldn't have come if he were not in the hospital. And yet that had nothing to do with the depth of her love for him. She loved him whether he was sick or healthy, strong or helpless. She loved him no matter what, and yet he thought it was only her overblown sense of duty that had brought her here and was making her say she loved him.

"That isn't fair," she protested helplessly. "Even if you can't walk, I should have the right to make my own choice. I love you. It doesn't matter to me if you can't walk."

"See?" he said contemptuously. "You're doing it again."

Suddenly Robyn's helplessness turned to cold fury. How dare he throw accusations at her and make her defend her love for him? It was he who had totally rejected her once, he who should answer for his abominable behavior. Here she was pouring out her love for him, trying desperately to convince him she loved him. For what? To satisfy his monumental ego? What difference did it make whether she loved him or not? He didn't love her!

She squared her shoulders abruptly. "Have you filed for the divorce yet?"

"No. I've been a bit — ah — tied up, as you might have noticed," he answered sardonically.

"Do you want me to file and get the legal processes started?"

He shrugged. "Suit yourself. I suppose it would be the quickest way."

Robyn swallowed convulsively, struggling to keep her composure. "Very well then," she managed to say. "I'll probably need a copy of the prenuptial agreement."

He frowned. "I tore it up."

Robyn's composure cracked into surprise. "You did? Why?"

He hesitated, his voice little more than a mumble when he finally said, "Just a wild idea I had."

"Idea about what?"

He stared out the window again. "That maybe we could somehow make it together. But I realized I was wrong when you sneaked out the minute the funeral was over. You were free and you could hardly wait to escape and enjoy your freedom."

Robyn felt dazed again, as if things were turning all topsy-turvy around her. "But that isn't true," she protested. "I left because I thought you and Shauna — I couldn't stand to stay around while you and she were — You never said anything!"

"I told you just before you walked out that I wanted to talk to you. But you had other things on your mind, as I recall."

"You could have tried to reach me later."

"Do you think I'd try to trap you into

taking care of a cripple? I'd already trapped you into a marriage you obviously detested."

"I loved you. I still do." She shook her head helplessly. "Why are you doing this to me? I don't understand."

"You don't love me. You only feel sorry —"

"I threw myself at you one night and you rejected me!" The humiliating admission made Robyn turn her head away, but Trev's words made her whirl back.

"And you rejected me on our wedding night!"

"That was different," Robyn retorted. "You didn't love me. You only wanted me because I — I was available. Someone to amuse yourself with as long as you were caught in a trap."

"Which is exactly the same reason you came to me," Trev pointed out grimly. "A 'fringe benefit' I believe you called it."

Yes, it was what she had said, Robyn agreed silently. But it wasn't true. She had thrown herself at him for one reason, and one reason only. Because she loved him.

"Okay, I'll admit it," Trev said slowly. "When we went through that marriage ceremony, I had two things on my mind. One was making Grandma happy before she died. The other was wanting you on a pretty much physical basis." He hesitated, then went on in an almost puzzled voice. "But there was something else too. Something I perhaps didn't recognize because I'd never felt it before. Or maybe I was afraid to recognize it. It started the very first time I saw you on the beach struggling to save that damn bird. I felt it again that time I brought you back to your house and Larry was there, acting as if he owned you. And he was still there when I went back later. I was really shaken up. I'd never felt that way about any woman before."

Robyn just looked at him, wide-eyed, uncertain what he was saying. "But if you felt something for me, why did you turn away from me and reject me that night?" she asked, bewildered. Then as the hurt and humiliation of that terrible night flooded back to her, her voice dropped almost to a whisper. "You treated me as if you couldn't stand to touch me. As if I were repugnant to you."

He shook his head. "No," he said flatly. "I wanted you more than I've ever wanted anything or anyone in my life."

"You chose a strange way to show it," Robyn said bitterly.

"Perhaps I did," he agreed slowly. "But that night, for the first time in my life, I felt something that was more than purely male instinct. I wanted more from you than just desire, using *me* as a 'fringe benefit.' Just sex wasn't enough, I wanted your love."

Robyn's bewilderment returned. "You looked at me with such contempt. I —"

"It wasn't contempt for you," he broke in harshly. "It was contempt for myself. I heard my own words coming from you about how we might as well get something for ourselves out of the marriage we were trapped in. I realized how cold-blooded and meaningless they were. I knew then that I didn't want anything less than your love. But I also realized I'd messed things up so badly that you could never love me."

Robyn shook her head. "I felt humiliated. Hurt beyond words. But I loved you so much I wanted you on any terms." She hesitated before adding softly, "I still do."

"You're willing to have me on any terms?"

Her hopes suddenly rose as the reasons for his humiliating rejection of her that night became clear. "Yes! I love you." She hesitated. "And you're saying, I *think* you're saying, you care for me too."

"I love you," he said. But it was not a happy or joyous statement. It was a stony, almost angry admission, and his face had a set, detached expression. "You should never have come here."

"But I don't understand!" Robyn cried,

emotions plummeting again. "I love you. You say you love me. Why shouldn't I have come?"

"Because I intended to come back to you when this was all over, when I was on my feet and healthy, and tell you I loved you and see if we couldn't somehow start all over. I didn't want you to see me like this because I knew you'd do just what you're doing. Saying you love me just because you feel sorry for me, because you feel a duty to take care of me because I'm like some stranded seagull. And I will not have you under those conditions!"

Robyn stared at him, angry and frustrated by his stubbornness. He was saying he loved her, and she certainly loved him. And yet he was throwing up this insurmountable barrier between them. "Yes, I do feel sorry for you!" she stormed angrily. "I feel sorry for you because you're stubborn and hardheaded and unable to see that I really love you, that my feelings have nothing to do with duty or a sense of responsibility. Sorry because you are obstinate and what your grandmother would probably have called just plain pigheaded!"

A flash of anger glittered in his blue eyes and his chiseled lips compressed into a harsh line. "Do you say such sweet things to every man you're in love with?"

"If you want to be rid of me then *you'll* have to divorce *me*," Robyn said firmly. "I can be stubborn too. You can't get up out of that bed to divorce me, so I guess you're just stuck with me." She braced her legs and folded her arms determinedly.

She felt a stir of alarm as he reached for the blue robe hanging by his bed. He yanked it around his shoulders and tied the rope cord at his waist. Then he flung the covers aside and hung his feet over the side of the bed.

"What are you doing?" Robyn cried, aghast. She ran to him, reaching out to grab him as his feet touched the floor. "You mustn't —"

"Don't help me!"

He brushed her hand aside and stood up. He took a few steps, pausing at the foot of the bed to eye her challengingly, then continuing on until he was standing by the window. He turned to face her.

"See? I'm not helpless. For a while I thought I would be. But the operation on my back was a success and I've been undergoing physical therapy treatments. I may have a slight permanent limp, but that is all. I'll be out of here in a week or two. You're free. You don't have to hang around to take care of me. So go on, go home. Get out."

Robyn just stood there, astonished and shaken. Even his paleness and the robe and hospital pajamas couldn't conceal his rugged masculinity, that air of raw maleness just beneath the surface that had always touched something deep and primitive within her. A muscle twitched spasmodically beneath that thin scar on his jaw.

"I love you," she said helplessly. "You're stubborn and infuriating. But I love you."

There was an odd expression in his intense blue eyes. "Don't keep saying that if you don't mean it because —"

He stopped without finishing the sentence. He took a determined stride toward her, then another. She wanted to run to him again, wanted to throw her arms around him, but she didn't. She forced herself to stand rigidly motionless as his strength and assurance seemed to increase with each step.

Then his arms were around her and his mouth found hers and claimed it in a kiss that ravished her mind and senses, awakened those same longings that only he had ever aroused.

When he finally lifted his mouth from hers, his eyes looked deep into hers. "I don't need you to take care of me," he said almost fiercely. "But I do need and want your love. For always. Because I love you. And this time," his voice was husky as he held her eyes in his smouldering blue gaze, "and this time, I shall make certain that we have a real wedding night."

The employees of Thorndike Press hope you have enjoyed this Large Print book. All our Large Print titles are designed for easy reading, and all our books are made to last. Other Thorndike Press Large Print books are available at your library, through selected bookstores, or directly from us.

For information about titles, please call:

(800) 223-1244
(800) 223-6121

To share your comments, please write:

Publisher
Thorndike Press
295 Kennedy Memorial Drive
Waterville, ME 04901